Q

and

SADE

D1522007

A COMPTON LOVE STORY

JADE JONES

&

PEBBLES STARR

www.jadedpublications.com

TO BE NOTIFIED OF NEW RELEASES, CONTESTS, GIVEAWAYS,

AND BOOK SIGNINGS IN YOUR AREA, TEXT **BOOKS** TO 44144

This novel is a work of fiction. Any reference to real people, events, establishments, or locales is intended only to give the fiction a sense of reality and authenticity. Other names, characters, and incidents occurring in the work are either the product of the author's imagination or are used fictitiously, as are those fictionalized events and events that involve real persons. Any character that happens to share the name of a person who is any acquaintance of the author, past or present, is purely coincidental and is in no way intended to be an actual account involving that person.

Copyright © 2017

LOOSELY BASED ON TRUE EVENTS

1

Sade

2000

"Maybe I want a nigga who ain't good."

—*Jayda*

Nelly's *"Country Grammar"* poured through the speakers of The Shark Bar on a Saturday night. The place was busier than a $2 whore on Friday night, and with so many people in one building, we had to forcefully squeeze our way to the bar just to get a drink.

Jayda and I were at All-Star Weekend Party in Oakland, California, surrounded by West Coast, Texas, Seattle and Vegas niggas. It was ironically, Valentine's Day and there was no shortage of men to go around. For my homegirl, this was the ideal setting, but for me, I felt totally out of place. I didn't do mixie shit like this, but as Jayda had suggested, a change of scenery wouldn't hurt. So, I decided to step outside my comfort zone, and turn up for the new millennium.

All of a sudden, a guy pinched my ass. "Aye, mamí, what'chu on tonight? How much to let me slide up in that raw?"

I reached in my bag and grabbed my can of mace. "How 'bout a trip to the hospital!" I spat at him, finger on the trigger ready to destroy his retinas. I wasn't playing with these forward ass niggas, and I sure as hell wasn't one to be groped on.

The nigga quickly scurried off, sparing himself a hefty medical bill.

"I can't believe I let you drag me here, bitch," I said, tugging on my denim skirt for what seemed like the hundredth time. The material stopped just a few inches above my knees but I still felt underdressed. Maybe that's why these niggas thought it was okay to grab on me. Because I let Jayda play dress-up since she claimed I was incapable of dressing up on my own. Normally, I rocked a pair of jeans and Chuck Taylors, but she wouldn't dare let my ass out of the hotel wearing that.

"Bitch, I wasn't coming solo. I had no choice but to bring you along. You know I wanted to see Romello." He was an underground rapper whose music she loved. He was also scheduled to perform later on tonight.

"Bitch, I doubt Romello wants to see you," I muttered.

Jayda gave me the finger, knowing damn well it was the truth. She was a pretty, chocolate girl with soft brown eyes, and a signature ponytail that she always wore up high. Smooth baby hairs aligned her edges, and I often told her she resembled a porcelain doll. At 5'5, she was slightly chubby, but carried it well because of her curves.

We were both 20, and Jayda was the closest thing I had to a sister. We met at a photography workshop at the New York Film Academy, and had been inseparable ever since. Our families were close, and her mother treated me as if I were her own. Like mine, her parents were good, upstanding folks, but that still didn't change Jayda's preference for street niggas. She had a serious penchant for bad boys—and Romello fit the bill perfectly.

At 6'3 and a solid 200 lbs., he was light-skinned, had good hair, and a broad football player's build. He was a pretty boy and all the bitches in Cali wanted him. Back in the day, he played college ball, but a torn ACL changed his path, and from there he turned to the streets.

A couple years ago, he started rapping, but he had yet to take off. He was a self-proclaimed pimp. Last year, he and Jayda met at his EP release party, and she'd been smitten by his ass ever since. She was what they called a "Stan". She went to all of his local performances and even managed to swing this All-Star trip just to see him.

Ignoring my snarky comeback, she pointed over towards his section. "Look, bitch! There he is! Looking like a fucking snack on a stick!"

Halfway across the club, I spotted Romello, surrounded by a bunch of people. They were all huddled around him like a bunch of thirsty ass groupies.

You would think this nigga was God himself, I thought.

Drunk off of his hood-fame, he started popping bottles, and pouring champagne all over his groupies. All eyes were on him, and he was loving the attention. He wanted everyone to know he had a bag, and some bad bitches that helped him secure it. The nigga thought he looked cool, but all I saw was a dumb ass.

"Come on! Let's go over there!" Jayda insisted.

"Don't you think he got enough bitches in his face?"

"Two more won't hurt." Jayda grabbed my wrist and tugged me along—

WHAM!

Too distracted by her shenanigans to pay attention, I ran smack into a tall, slender nigga with braids. The contents in his plastic cup spilled all over his red Golden State Warriors jersey.

"GOTDAMN, BITCH! The fuck is you doing?! You tripping!" he yelled. "You realize how much this shit cost???"

Floored at the disrespect, I gaped silently at him, unable to respond. I knew exactly who he was right away. Q's name rang bells in the streets, as well as the dangerous criminal organization that he ran. He was in his early 20s, but he was already an established street legend. A lot of people had respect for him, because he made sure his hood ate. A lot of folks that made it outta Compton couldn't say that, Romello was case in point. They usually blew up, and forgot about the little people, but not Q. He kept it solid in the streets, and that's why everyone respected him. He got money and he was an animal in the streets. Growing up, me and every girl in Compton used to have a crush on this nigga. He always good looking with long pretty hair that he either kept braided or pulled back into a ponytail. We dreamed of him giving us the time of day, but he paid our young asses no mind. He was too busy chasing fast money and fast women.

"And you a rude ass bitch, too! They ain't teach you no manners out in East Oakland??? On blood, I should smack the fuckin' apology outta you!"

His rant quickly snapped me from my thoughts. "First off, I ain't from East Oakland, nigga! I'm from Compton! And secondly, you put your muthafuckin' hands on me, I'll be the last bitch you ever touch!" My father worked directly under the sheriff of Compton, so I had no problem making sure of that. I didn't give a fuck about his street status or the fact that I used to like him. I wasn't going to let anyone put their hands on me.

The space between us was fraught with tension, and suddenly, the guy who was with him stepped in. "Damn, Q! Let her know that shit is official! It's only fifty of them bitches made, period!" he said. "Say hoe, you must gon' buy him a new one."

"It's always an extra bum ass nigga that got something to say! Nigga, I ain't spill nothing on you! I spilled it on him, so fuck you!" I flipped his ass off for being an instigator. "How's that for a hoe?"

"I can bet my trap you gon' apologize!" Q threatened. "I put that on my set, my son, and everything...Oh, best believe I'mma get a muthafuckin' apology!"

His instigating friend continued to laugh as Q stared daggers at me. He was hot as fuck about his jersey, awaiting some sort of atonement, but an apology was the last thing he would get from me. I didn't give a damn how dangerous they looked. I wasn't about to let their asses disrespect me.

"I don't have an apology for your ass. But here's something I *do* have." I turned my middle finger towards him. "How 'bout that?"

He tried to recover his ego. "Fuck you talking to?! Who you talking to like that? Yo, you actin' real disrespectful right now, bitch. You must not know who the fuck I am!"

Q's friend placed a hand to his chest to stop him from overreacting. He was obviously accustomed to his blustery explosions of rage. "Chill out, champ. Don't do no brazy shit."

"Nah, I'm good. I'm cool. I'mma stall her out. I ain't gon' let her see the bad side of me...yet" He threatened while glaring at me from behind his homeboys extended forearm.

"Trust me. We already seeing it," Jayda said, finally coming to my defense. "Ya'll niggas need to fall the fuck back! You know damn well she ain't mean to spill that shit."

"Yeah, well, she ain't mean to pay attention to where the fuck she was going either! Now my shit is all fucked up! And on top of that, the silly bitch can't even apologize!"

"You got one more time to call me a bitch, and you gon' catch these hands like the flu."

"Chill, Sade. This nigga ain't worth making a scene..."

With a look of cool distaste, Q and his friend walked off, but not before his friend stole a quick glance at Jayda's ass.

"Bitch, I wouldn't be making a scene if your ass hadn't dragged me here!" I pointed to Romello's section, where 2 white bitches and a sista were kissing his feet in a worshipping fashion. He obviously thought he was a god of some sort, but in reality, he was just as clowned out as the nigga I'd bumped into. "This nigga so fucking burnt out. I don't know who's worse. Him or the silly ass bitches he got on the floor! Look at 'em. Kissing his muthafuckin' dirty ass." I shook my head in disgust. "You seriously have no self-worth doing some trifling ass shit like that. Then again, these the same silly ass hoes paying a Pimp in the first place." I paused my breathless rant to shake my head at them in pity. It was clear that the women had no morals or principles of any kind. "He ain't a God. Does that weak ass shit make him feel like he's that nigga??"

"Bitch, he *is* that nigga! Plus, he ain't got no gun to them hoes' heads. So, if anyone's weak, it's them, not him."

Jayda was always defending this clown, and I was really beginning to get sick of it. "Just 'cuz he a hood nigga, don't mean he a good nigga."

"Maybe I want a nigga who ain't good," she giggled.

"Well, you go right ahead. 'Cuz I sure as shit ain't." Folding my arms, I shook my head at Romello. I hated the way he publicly treated women, and what's more, I hated his shitty music. It was downright degrading and so was he. Honestly, I didn't know what the hell Jayda saw in this fool. "You wanna talk about making a scene...If anybody's making a scene, it's *that* clown ass nigga."

Speaking of clown ass nigga, I shot an evil glare at the fake, corner store jersey-wearing guy from earlier. If looks could kill, he would've been dead on the spot. He was still shaking his head in frustration, undoubtedly ticked off about his shirt.

"You such an evil bitch, Sade!" Jayda yelled over the music. She could no longer suppress her amusement as she cracked up with laughter. "On me, I can't believe you really told him that shit! You used to be on that nigga's dick back in the day, too. You so muthafuckin' burnt out, bitch! You're going straight to Hell's VIP section."

"I was just talking shit, but you see how tight he got about it," I said. "Only a hit dog will holler." Glancing back over in his direction, I shot him one final look of disapproval.

He may've been a hot-tempered, possibly violent asshole, but the nigga was finer than a muthafucka. Soft caramel skin, greenish-gray eyes, thick, pussy-sucking lips, and a swagger that left me tingling all over. It was obvious that the crush from my youth had followed me into adulthood.

Q looked even better than he did back then. He was distinctively handsome, sporting a teardrop under his right eye, and the words *Cedar Block Piru* tatted across his neck in bold cursive. He wasn't quite stocky, but he wasn't a lil' nigga, either, and he had a powerful presence about him that shook the most solid of foundations.

He was banging blood, and always wore his color proudly. His homie was with the shits too, because he had CK tatted on his face, which stood for Crip Killer. They were members of one of the most feared drug gangs in the nation. And they had all the qualities of the guys my father taught me to avoid...and yet, something about Q intrigued the hell out of me.

All that banging and shit is just a one-way ticket to a cheap ass funeral, my father would often say. He'd grown a strong resentment for gang-bangers after my mom was murdered during a store robbery. The suspects were never found but he believed they were gang bangers.

A slow smile crept across my face as I watched Q disappear into the crowd. Like Jayda, I too, had a weakness for bad boys—even after what happened to my mom. My father always said that he'd kill me if I ever ended up with one of them. I always tried to honor my father's wishes, but good guys were so boring. Take my ex, Frederick for example. He came from money, went to college and worked in his father's law firm. He was as straight-laced as they came, and my father had all but planned our wedding. I gave him 8 months of my life, but when I wouldn't give up the goods, he got frustrated and bounced. But if all bad boys looked as good as Q, then I was surely headed to an early grave.

2

Q

"I swear to God, I'mma put a bounty on all them niggas heads!"

—*Q*

Can't believe this shit. I sulked in anger as I wiped at the stain on my tee. Not to mention the mouth on shorty that caused it, then, to add insult to injury, the bitch couldn't even apologize. Her trifling ass behavior was totally uncalled for, considering she was the one in the wrong.

She better be lucky she cute, I huffed. Little did she know, that was the *only* muthafuckin' thing that saved her lil' pretty ass.

Sade had a nice visual. With her smooth brown, skin, gentle eyes and baby face, she was truly a sight to behold. She didn't have much in the ass department, but what she lacked, she made up for with a busty bosom. Her fiery and rebellious attitude only made her more attractive. Secretly, I admired her and the way she stood up to me.

In all my years of banging, a nigga had never been talked to in such a way. The bitch had a mouth on her. A mouth that had absolutely no filter. She obviously didn't know how dangerous of a nigga I was, 'cuz if she did she wouldn't have been so quick to risk her life.

She better be damn lucky she's cute and from my hood.

Though Sade had infuriated me, she'd also managed to somewhat intrigue me. Her feisty demeanor, and razor sharp tongue were a welcoming surprise, as well as a turn on. Then again, everything about her fine ass was a turn on. But what I found most appealing was her unwillingness to back down. She was harder than a lot of these niggas, 'cuz nobody talked to a YG like that and lived to tell about it.

Looking back over my shoulder, I spotted her at the bar conversing with her girl. I laughed inside when I realized she was probably still dogging my ass.

"Blood, that bitch was funny as fuck!" LaMar laughed.

"Nah, she was *acting* funny as fuck."

"Facts, but aye, that's what'chu need right there, lil' homie."

"What? Another fucking headache? Nah, I don't need that shit. Besides...she ain't 'een my type for real," I lied.

"Muthafucka, have you saw yo baby momma? You don't have a muthafuckin' type!" he laughed.

LaMar was my day one, my shooter. He put the H in Hitta. At 5'10, he was around the same height as me, and we shared the same complexion, and body build. He was two years older than me at 23, and people often thought we were related. The only difference was that I wore braids, and he rocked nappy freeform dreads. I figured we'd been hanging together so long that our muthafuckin' asses started resembling each other.

We ate off the same plate, grew up in the same hood, and we were as thick as thieves. He was my partner in crime in every aspect of the game. Drugs, cars, hoes, and every other hustle we were dick deep in. If there was anyone I could count on, it was him. A lot of these niggas talked that loyalty shit, but with L, it wasn't just a word. The nigga took fades for me, as well as cases for me, and he was as real as they came.

"Fuck outta here, nigga. I *do* have a type, and it sure as shit ain't that!" I told him. "Just 'cuz you like to stick yo dick in anything, doesn't mean a fly nigga like me don't have standards. And trust me, a smart-mouthed bitch like that *definitely* doesn't meet them!"

"Yeah, that's what'chu say, homie..." Lamar paused, and his smile faded. "Oh shit, there go our boys right there. It's game time," He said, giving me the heads up.

The niggas we were delivering to were in a section not too far from us. Normally, I had runners to do this type of shit, but since the bread was right, I made the exception. This specific client was a long-term buyer of mine, as well as a world-famous music producer. I sold to many A-listers, but this one in particular always purchased in large quantities, so I made the coke run with my shooter to meet the coke buyer in person. With so much money at stake, I wasn't about to take any chances. Shit had to be perfect.

"Soren, my man. Good to see you," I said, dapping up the hottest producer out right now. He was a solid, bulky dude with dreads to his waist, and a burn scar across his cheek. He was draped in heavy ass chains and Cuban links, and designer from head to toe. I would've asked how he was living, but from the look of things, he was living pretty damn good.

I wasn't with all that flashy shit. Getting rich the illegal way, you had to stay off the radar as much as possible. I liked nice things and all, but the less attention I drew, the better. Everyone knew success breeds haters. When enemies came in numbers, you had to play by the street rules. I knew I had the best, so there were always niggas gunning for me. They were like hyenas trying to overthrow the lion. Competition from other dealers was fierce, but finding a supplier with high quality snow was rare. There was only one place you could get cocaine this good and that was through me.

I'd been selling drugs damn near my whole life, so I was a vet when it came to this shit. I had the game on lock right now, always playing defense more than I was offense.

"Shit, changing the game one track at a time," he said. "Thanks for making that drive."

Getting caught with just 4 ounces held a maximum of 4 years, and in my duffel bag was 25 pounds of cocaine, so you do the math. Me and LaMar were taking a big risk by coming here, but big risks often came with even bigger rewards.

"Oh, no doubt. You know how we do," I said, handing him the duffel bag.

Soren peeked inside, and smiled at the purest cocaine money could buy. Our shit was worth more than gold, but like a wise man once said *'Price is what you pay, value is what you get.'*

"Everything looking good. That chicken right," he said. He then signaled for his man to hand over a large duffle bag. Inside was about half a million dollars. I opened the bag to make sure it was no funny business, then we made the exchange and shook hands.

"As always, it was a pleasure doing business with you."

LaMar and I left his section, and I couldn't help but notice the smirk that was lingering on his face. "Fuck is so funny?" I asked.

"Bitch said you got that shit from the corner shop." He couldn't stop laughing. "Aye, she straight played the fuck outta you, homie. You need that back fade, on Piru. Buzzo, you took more Ls than the DMV gives out!"

I shoved the heavy ass duffel bag into his arms, shutting his ass up instantly. "Man, get up off that bitch She was on some other shit."

"Aye, while we on the subject of some other shit...what the fuck is this bozo doing?" We were on our way out the door when LaMar pointed to a VIP section. A pack of groupies was huddled around a flashy nigga draped in chains.

I scoffed in disgust once I realized who it was. Romello, the Ladies Man. I figured his shit must've cleared yesterday, 'cuz the nigga was acting like new money. "He out here making the set look bad. That's what the fuck he doing."

The nigga swore up and down he was banging blood, but everyone knew he wasn't. If anything, he was just a hood nigga with a few coins and even fewer connects. The muthafucka wanted to be down so bad, but he wasn't really 'bout that street shit. He just talked about the streets, and put on for his "fans". Me and my niggas were real trappers. We were really living the shit these fake ass niggas rapped about.

"Real P shit! WEST UP OR VEST UP!" Romello and his crew chanted the hook to one of his weak ass songs.

"The pussification is real," LaMar said. "This nigga rather floss than boss. What kinda bullshit he on?"

"That nigga gone fuck around and get his wings clipped, trying to be fly and shit." Money couldn't buy you clout. It couldn't buy you reputation, and it damn sure couldn't buy you heart. Romello failed to realize that shit.

"Blood brazy, man," LaMar said, shaking his head. "Is this what stomp down izm has come to?"

"Man, these lames take the value out the game and themselves. On god, that nigga ain't no real pimp," I said.

"Muthafucka said 'on god'." LaMar broke out laughing. "Nigga, real bloods know it's in you not on you, and he clearly don't got it in him." Suddenly, his eyes grew big. "Hold up, fam…I could be trippin', but ain't that Camari hoe ass on the ground???"

I did an automatic double take, and sure enough there she was. My baby momma on her hands and knees, kissing his shoes, like he was her savior.

This silly bitch done lost the last bit of mind she has left.

She was already a deadbeat when it came to taking care of our son. She couldn't even buy him a pair of shoes, and yet here she was kissing this nigga Romello's. My body boiled with anger as I watched her make a fool of herself. Not only was she embarrassing herself; she was embarrassing me and everything I stood for. Everyone knew she was my baby momma, so her actions were a reflection of me.

I knew the bitch wasn't shit when I met her, but back then, she wasn't this out of control. Now at the point of no return, not even I could save her. She was more dedicated to her pimp than she was to being a parent, and that shit made me lose all respect for her. Still, I'd be damned if I let this shit go on any longer than it already had.

"CAMARI!" I yelled out. Before she could answer, I walked over and snatched her black ass up by her ponytail. "BITCH, STOP CROWNING THESE CLOWNS, AND GET'CHO SILLY ASS UP OFF THE FLOOR!" I hollered. "You can be in the club but can't check on ya son?! No calls, no visit! But you out! Seems like your priorities are all fucked up!"

"Get the fuck off me, Q!" she screamed, not wanting to hear any of it. Her eyes were glassy and red-rimmed, and she had coke residue in the corner of her nose. "My muthafuckin' priorities ain't got shit to do with you or Peace. So mind yo fucking business and leave me to mine!" Hearing her say that our son wasn't a priority made me want to choke her ass out right here in this crowded night club.

"Bitch, you *are* my fucking business! And I ain't leaving you no gotdamn where!! Look at what the fuck you doing!!! And for what???"

"What I do, and *why* I do it is no concern to you!"

Unable to refrain myself any longer, I seized her by the throat, lifting her off of her feet.

"Wait! Hold on! The fuck is you doing with my property, homie?!" Romello interjected.

"*Yo property*?! Bitch nigga, this is the mother of my son! She has *always* been my property!"

Romello responded by pulling out a switchblade. "Well, guess yo lease done ended, muthafucka!"

No sooner than he pulled out the blade, I grabbed a bottle and launched it at his head. He ducked and it cracked his homeboy instead, and from there, shit was on and popping. Hopping over the table, LaMar cracked Romello in the head with the duffel bag. He was always the first to go whenever some shit jumped off.

WHAP!

Romello lost his footing and crashed into his groupies. He barely had a chance to retaliate before his partners swooped in to help. I wasted no time doing the same, as I swung on one of his boys. Blow for blow, I held my own against two niggas that were twice my size.

WHAP!

WHAP!

WHAP!

I dropped the biggest with a few body shots, then pieced his friend with a blow to the kidney. Romello's entourage quickly jumped in, as well as the Bloods that knew me from the hood. We had walked in 2-deep, but shit was still a go. We had snipers in the shadows wherever we went. They were like our guardian angels, and always came through when we needed them to.

Together, me and the homies ran through them niggas without breaking a sweat. We were mopping the floor with their asses when Camari started pepper spraying niggas. Shortly after, a riot broke out, and before security could intervene, shots went off.

POP!

POP!

POP!

POP!

A stampede quickly erupted, with folks running in every which direction. Ducking for cover, I made sure to keep my head down to avoid being hit. From the floor, I couldn't see who was shooting, but they had that bitch lit up like the 4th of July.

POP!

POP!

POP!

They were letting that thing go crazy. Screaming people pushed to get out of the club, and in the midst of all the chaos, I somehow got split up from my bro. Knowing LaMar and his capabilities, I wasn't too worried about him, but Camari, however, was a whole other story. The bitch may've been a crackhead ass hooker, but she was still the mother of my son, and I begrudgingly cared about her well-being.

Suddenly, I spotted Camari a few feet away, cowering behind a sofa. Rushing over, I grabbed her hand and darted through the mass of people. Once we were outside, I turned around to make sure she was okay and—

"GET THE FUCK OFF ME!"

The chick who spilled the drink on me earlier had pushed the shit out of me.

"WHAT THE HELL ARE YOU DOING??? MY GIRL IS STILL IN THERE!" she screamed.

Up until this point, I hadn't realized that I'd grabbed the wrong chick. She and Camari both had ponytails, so it was easy to confuse the two.

"Q!"

Suddenly, LaMar came running out of the building, carrying Camari. He still had the duffel bag on his shoulder, but the money was the least of my worries. Hit with a wave of panic, I rushed over to make sure my baby momma was good. "Is she a'ight? Is she hit?" I asked, surveying her body for wounds. "I swear to God, I'mma put a bounty on all them niggas heads!"

"She good, fam. She just twisted her ankle."

"I didn't twist my ankle! It was trampled over!" she yelled.

"Well, you brought this shit on yaself!"

"Nah, nigga, you brought this shit to me! What I was doing was my muthafuckin' business!" she argued. "It had nothing to do with your ass!"

"Bitch, as long as I'm breathing yo business *is* my business! You the mother of my child, and a reflection of me! You out here wildin' and shit, knowing my name ring bells! Man, that shit is disrespectful as fuck! Then on top of that, you giving this clown ass nigga the money and attention you should be giving to your son! But that only shows what type of bitch you are! A nothing ass dick-sucking hoe!"

"*JAYDA*!! OH MY GOD! SOMEONE CALL 911!!!!"

My attention shifted to a woman whose shirt was covered in blood. It was Sade's friend, and she'd been hit by one of the stray bullets meant for me.

Turning to LaMar, I instructed for him to take Camari back to my room. I couldn't just leave the situation in the present state that it was in. After all, it was my fault that shit had even gone down like this. I just couldn't take seeing Camari on her hands and knees like that, embarrassing me. If there was anyone who she should've placed on a pedestal, it was the muthafuckin' son that she neglected.

"Is she a'ight?" I asked Sade, who was looking at her bleeding friend in horror. Pulling out my bandana, I handed it to her to stop the blood flow. "Here, take this—"

"Look, we don't need shit else from you, okay!" There was a strained expression on her face as she pointed a finger at me. "You've already caused more than enough trouble! Look around you! This is all your gotdamn fault! If you wanna help somebody, help your muthafuckin' self!" She said with tears streaming down her face.

Containing my anger, I bit my tongue in an attempt to keep my cool. I then looked around and took in everything that was happening around me. People were frantically searching for their cars, and in the distance, I could hear sirens approaching. As guilty as I felt about the people that were hurt, I didn't feel much remorse. But now wasn't the time to be heartless when all this shit was kinda my fault.

I should have smoked that nigga Romello, and right now that was my only regret. Speaking of Romello, his shooter was escorted out in handcuffs.

"Bitch ass nigga on blood, you a stain! We on you, fuck nigga!" Romello yelled at me. "We on you, and anybody that fuck with you!"

"Aye, you got yo card pulled, pussy nigga. But it's cool. I'mma see you around."

"You can see me now, bitch ass nigga. Running from a fade, you know this ain't what you want!" Romello threatened. "On God, I'mma catch yo ass in public! You got niggas on yo head now, homeboy!"

I ain't like the way the fuck nigga was talking. He was getting reckless with his shit 'cuz he knew police was around. As bad as I wanted to rock that nigga to sleep, I somehow remained collected. Instead of responding to his weak ass threats, I went back to helping Sade. We could bang it out later, and may the best man win. "Here. This'll help with the bleeding." I tied my bandana tightly around Jayda's arm. Sade looked pissed that I'd taken it upon myself to step in, but she kept her cool considering the circumstances.

"You gon' be alright, bitch, stop being so dramatic," she laughed through tears.

"You're the one who's crying," Jayda pointed out.

Sade quickly wiped her tears and laughed. She felt a little better knowing that her friend wasn't seriously injured, and so did I. "The ambulance is on the way. I can hear them now."

When they finally arrived, Jayda was one of 3 others treated for minor injuries. Luckily, there were no casualties. Had there been, I might've carried a guilty conscience. From a distance, I watched as Jayda was packed into an ambulance. Sade asked if she could ride with her friend, but was turned away. They simply didn't have the room for her, and she would have to follow them to the hospital.

Stranded on the curb, I waited for her to leave and follow them, but instead she rummaged through her purse, as if looking for something she needed. After several minutes of aimless searching, I finally realized something was wrong.

Making my way over, I asked if everything was okay. "Aye, you good?"

All of a sudden, she snapped on a nigga. "Do I look like I'm good??"

Because of the situation, I decided to give her ass another pass. But if she continued talking crazy, I couldn't be held accountable for smacking the fire up out her ass.

"I see you're upset. How can I fix that?" My tone softened as I tried to sympathize with her. "Is there something I can do?"

The look she gave implied that there wasn't. "I think you've done enough," she said grimly. "Besides, Jayda has the car keys, so unless you can magically pull them out of your ass, then no! There's not a damn thing you can do."

There was no excuse for such fucked up manners. After all, she'd bumped into me. "Aye, say, I'mma need you to ease the fuck up. I'm only tryin' to help yo muthafuckin' ass, so you can calm down with all that shit. Now do you need this ride to the telly or nah?"

"I'm not going back to the hotel—or anywhere with your muthafuckin' ass! And why the hell would I go back to the room anyway after everything that just happened?

The only place I'm going is to the hospital to check on my girl. And the last person I want accompanying me is you!"

I knew she was in an irritable state, but I didn't follow her reasoning. "All this talking, we could be halfway there."

"Tuh! Nigga, please...I'd rather walk from Slauson to Boston!"

Her feelings were translated through her expression. She had a growing hatred for me, and had no problem expressing it. The bitch had a funky ass attitude...but that's what made her even sexier. On the real, I just wanted to grab and kiss her lil' pretty, mean ass.

"Damn, it's like that? Nigga just trying to look out, but you actin' like a muthafucka finna rape you."

"Trust me. It's not an act!" she shot back. "I saw that fight you started in there! And to be honest, I want nothing to do with your troublesome ass!"

"*Troublesome*? How the fuck you figure *I'm* troublesome??" Now my dignity was offended. "You don't 'een know what the fuck going on, so don't speak on some shit like it's facts."

"You wanna talk about *facts*?? Nigga, you were nothing but trouble from the moment I bumped into you! The *fact* is, you're nothing but a sorry ass, corner store jersey-wearing, gang banging piece of shit!"

I immediately resisted the impulse to slap her. As fine as she was, I forgot that attraction in an instant. "I'll be all that, but at least I gotta way home! Find ya own fucking ride, bum ass bitch!"

"FUCK YOU!" she yelled, animosity brewing in her tone.

"Nah, fuck you, broke ass hoe!"

Finally fed up with the bullshit, I walked away and left her to brood alone. If I stayed a second longer, I was liable to put her fucking ass in the hospital, too. The bitch had a muthafuckin' mouth on her, and she was about to fuck around and get that shit split open.

I also knew that a nigga had to have her.

Sade had just pulled out her Nokia to call up a cab, when I pulled my red Viper alongside her. Because of the tint, she couldn't see who was in it, but something told me she already knew.

I rolled my window down, and she immediately caught an attitude. "What do you want? I told you that I'm not getting in your car!"

"You ain't got no choice. Ain't no taxis coming this way. It's too much going on, so just chill, and lemme take you where you gotta go."

With all of the commotion going on, it'd be hard to catch a cab anywhere within a 5-mile radius of the club. People could get out, but no one could get in. Police had the entire perimeter blocked off.

Sade frowned at the thought of having to deal with me anymore than she already had...but it wasn't like she had much of a choice. I wasn't going to let her ass walk the streets of Oakland alone. That just wasn't in my repertoire.

"Look, I'm sorry. I know I said some bullshit to you. And we might've got off to a rocky start, but I promise I ain't holdin' onto that. Just let me take you where you gotta go, and you'll never see or hear from me again," I said. "How does that sound?"

Sade thought about her options, or lack thereof. I guess something in the depth of my eyes made her trust me, because she finally accepted and walked over towards the car. "That sounds like a deal."

I leaned in and opened the passenger door for her. After muttering a thank you, she pulled her seatbelt on. OutKast's *"So Fresh, So Clean"* poured through the subwoofers in my red race car, and the inside was foggy as hell. I tried to pass her the blunt I was hitting, but she politely declined, wrinkling her nose.

I chuckled, amused by her innocence. She legit was a good girl. It'd been a long ass time since I met one of those.

3

Romello

"In my world, women equaled wealth."

—*Romello*

Kicking the door open to my hotel, I walked in my suite and slammed the door behind me. I was mad than a muthafucka that I didn't even get to perform, and because of that incident, the club owners refused to cut me a check. Not only did them niggas fuck up my evening, they'd also fucked up my revenue.

Swear these muthafuckas always hating on a young nigga. I may've lived my life more recklessly than others, but what gave them muthafuckas the right to judge me? Everybody out here trying to run it. I was simply trying to get it like the next man. What gave them the right to look down on me for pimping. So what if it wasn't a conventional hustle. That didn't take away from the fact that I was still a hustler. Niggas was just mad because they couldn't get to my level.

Temper flaring, I poured myself a shot of gin and took a seat on the living room sofa. I couldn't believe my night had ended like this. Lame ass niggas like Q hated to see another man shining. I should've burnt his bitch ass, but he wasn't worth the murder charge. I never did like that cocky ass nigga. He walked around with an undeserved sense of accomplishment. Like he was Nino Brown, or Big Meech, or some shit, but them niggas weren't really 'bout it. They were famous nobodies, and they hated to see a young nigga like me winning. I had tried to be down with them, but he laughed in my face. After that, I turned to pimping because that shit came easy to me. I was a chick magnet. A ladies' man. Had been all my life. I didn't have to run game on these hoes, because they basically flocked to a nigga. They saw the way me and my crew were living and they wanted a piece of it. And hating ass niggas like Q couldn't stand it.

They couldn't stand to see all of the beautiful bitches in my section. They couldn't stand to see me popping bottles. And contrary to popular belief, none of them bitches had to be coerced. I never told them hoes to get on the ground and start kissing a nigga's feet. They just did that shit on their own free will, not giving a fuck how anyone else felt about it.

I'd changed their muthafuckin' lives when I grabbed their dusty asses off the Blade. They were hoeing for pocket change before I came along and upgraded them. Like polishing off a trophy, I made them hoes look worth something and then put their asses to work. With me, they made 10 times as much as they did on their own, and their new clientele had a lot more money.

They were nobodies before I came and made them into somebodies. I took 'em all over the world, showed them the finer things in life, put designer on their backs, and provided them the best drugs to pump into their bodies, and for that they loved and cherished my ass.

Some people couldn't handle seeing that level of devotion and they got offended. They couldn't understand how a bitch could love a nigga that much and why she'd sacrifice her own pride. They couldn't understand how a young nigga like me had so much power and so much pussy at my disposal. They were always trying to piece some shit together. Meanwhile, I was taking flights and knocking a new bitch every night.

"Fuck them hating ass niggas." Turning on the TV, I rolled up a joint to take my mind off the bullshit and unwind. Old Super Bowl reruns were airing on ESPN.

Back in high school, I used to play offensive linebacker. I had dreams and aspirations of going to the NFL but I fucked around and got injured, which changed my whole game plan. I started pimping as a quick means of getting cash. I never expected it to bring me vast wealth, so I started rapping a few years later. It was my second passion after sports, and I needed this shit to take off.

"Daddy? What do you think of this?" Naytoma asked, twirling around in a metallic two-piece set. Her perky tits and fat ass were on full display. She was on her way to the upscale hotel bars and night clubs in West Hollywood, where all the ballers and rich people mingled. "I need your opinion on it."

I had to grab my dick on that shit. "Oh, I got an opinion for you."

At 19, Naytoma was my youngest moneymaker. She had that cum-fast body, and was a pretty white bitch with long, blonde hair, and my name tatted above her eyebrow. Of all my hoes, she brought home the most paper. She had that young, tight, comeback, and the niggas loved a big booty snow bunny.

"So, do you approve?" she asked, waiting on a response.

I curled my finger and beckoned her closer. Naytoma came over and I took in the sight of her. Gently running my fingers along her calve muscles, I admired the shape and smoothness of them. She had a nice ass and tits, but her legs were by far her best feature. She had long legs like the twin towers. I slid my hands up her mini-skirt and removed her panties. "Now, I do."

Naytoma strutted away, stuffing her panties inside her purse. Knowing her freaky ass clients, they would problem come in handy. A lot of people didn't respect the shit that I did. They viewed me as a predator, a womanizer, a whoremonger. But it wasn't those things that made me a player.

I had a finesse, a soft side, and good looks. I'd learned early on what the power of all three could accomplish. I've had bitches paying me since before pimping was even a thought. But it wasn't until I hit rock bottom that I began to take this shit serious. With no other options left, I put a wig on a pig and told her ass to get it. One hoe turned into two, and then eventually, the ball was rolling. Some slid and some stayed, but a few solid ones rode it out with me.

This was a mind game that not many males could play, and it couldn't and wouldn't work on a bitch that knew and valued her worth. Lucky for me, Camari, Naytoma, and Chelsie only valued the almighty dollar. Camari was the trillest of them all. If I had the gun, she had the clip. She was the first bitch I grabbed up, and she turned around and recruited the other 2.

In my world, women equaled wealth. Selling pussy wasn't all I had these bitches doing. When it came to the streets, I was a jack of all trades, who always saw the bigger picture. I had these bitches luring in the big money cats to help fund our expensive way of living.

All of this shit was setting me up to become a bigger boss. By the time my rap career took off, I'd already be a legend. Until then, I would continue stacking whore and blue faces, and using everyone as pawns in my rise to success. If a nigga had to pimp out every daughter in LA along the way, then so be it. I had to get this paper by any means necessary.

4

Sade

"That's only 'cuz you niggas drive us crazy."

—*Sade*

Neither Q, nor I felt an inclination to talk during the ride to the hospital. We simply rode in silence, grateful to finally be away from all of the chaos back at the club. The drive took less than fifteen minutes, and when we arrived, I was surprised to see Q take off his seatbelt.

"What are you doing? You don't have to come up," I told him.

"I know I don't have to. I want to. Like you said, this one is on me. Let me take care of shit. It's the least I can do."

Q pulled out a fat wad of cash, and I instantly frowned my face up. "Trust me, you don't have to do all that—"

"We'll let Jayda decide. Or do you run your friendships, too?"

"Q—"

"Look, I'mma keep it a buck with you. She wouldn't 'een have been involved in that shit if not for me. A man always takes accountability for his actions. So you gotta at least let me compensate for mine."

I respected the fact that he was a standup guy, so I left it at that. Ignoring my urge to argue any further, I climbed out the car and headed towards the entrance. Once inside, I greeted the receptionist and was instructed on where to find Jayda. As soon as we reached her room, I turned towards Q to say something, but he beat me to the punch.

"Go 'head. I'll be out here."

Grateful for his understanding, I dismissed myself and entered the room. The doctor had just snipped the last suture on Jayda's arm when I walked in. The bitch was seated on the hospital bed, with an uncharacteristically wide grin for someone who'd just been shot.

"Bitch, what the fuck got you smiling and shit?"

She laughed. "You mean *who*."

At this point, I wasn't even sure I wanted to know...but that didn't stop Jayda from telling me anyway.

"Romello sent someone up here to pay our hospital bills. He covered everyone's expenses that were injured in the shoot-out."

I snorted. "That's the least he could do. After all, he was the one who started it."

"Bitch, stop hating! That shit was hella sweet— regardless of how you may feel about him."

"So now that you're all patched up, can we get this car and bounce?"

"I'll get the car. You go ahead back to the room."

"Is this your slick way of trying to creep off to see Romello? Don't tell me that nigga invited you to his room or some shit."

"Bitch, not even. Quit tripping. I only said that 'cuz I see Q standing outside the door. You ain't slick, bitch. I was just trying to look out for you. I figured ya'll could chop it up on the way back to my room. No sense in me being shot *and* being a cock blocker. Do your thing. I'll catch back up with you at the hotel."

***

I found Q sitting on a bench outside of Jayda's room. "You don't have to worry about the bill. Apparently, Jayda's got it all under control."

Q must've sensed the agitation in my tone. "Everything good, ma? You seem irritated."

"No, I'm just tired. It's late, I'm drained. This has been the longest night of my life." I sighed dejectedly. "Look, I'll give you some gas money to take me back to my hotel room." I offered him, knowing it would be in vain.

"C'mon now, ma. You know the only thing I'm taking is that apology."

"You're still on that shit?" I asked him. "You didn't take me as someone who holds grudges?"

"And you ain't take me as a petty, stubborn broad. Say, what the fuck is yo sign, anyway?"

"I'm a Scorpio, if you must know."

Q shook his head. "Damn. Two Scorpios. A disastrous combination."

"So, you're a Scorpio, too. How interesting. But why you gotta say it like you've had some bad experiences."

"'Cuz that's facts. My baby momma a Scorpio. Ya'll bitches is crazy."

"That's only 'cuz you niggas drive us crazy."

"You driving me crazy right now, waiting on this muthafuckin' apology."

"Sorry...there...Are you happy now?" I offered him with a smug grin.

Q shrugged. "Shit could've been more heartfelt."

"Look, you barely even deserved that. I wasn't just in the wrong on my own, you know. After all, it takes two to tango," I reminded him.

"Yeah, and it's gon' take two muthafuckin' feet to walk home. Now do you want this muthafuckin' ride or nah?"

"Yes!" I answered, graciously. Lord knows, I didn't feel like waiting on a cab, or paying that high ass fare.

"A'ight then. Bring yo ass on." On the way to the car, Q went to open the passenger's door. "Here. Let me get that for you. Don't want you hurting yaself."

Oomf!

He damn near knocked me over by accident, but quickly caught me before I lost my footing.

"My bad, mamí."

I sucked my teeth. "Damn, you're clumsy as fuck. And you had the nerve to go off on me?"

"You know that mouth of yours gone get'chu fucked up."

***

Donell Jones' "*U Know What's Up*" played on low as we drove through the streets of Oakland towards the 3-

star hotel Jayda and I were staying at. With both of us working small gigs here and there, there was only so much luxury our meager budget could afford.

As I sat in his passenger seat, I felt a mixture of feelings. I was beyond attracted to Q, but his ego, I could do without. Still, I appreciated him for sticking around to make sure me and my girl were good, especially when he didn't have to. Perhaps, under all that gruff exterior was really a great, big heart.

Speaking of his heart, I became curious about his love life. Did he have a girl? Was she the mother of the son he'd mentioned in the club? What type of women was he attracted to?

I'm digging you, I'm feeling you...

And you know what's up...

Said I'm big on you and I'm wanting you...

So, tell me what's up...

Donell Jones' sweet, melodic voice alleviated some of the tension between us. Q hadn't spoken a word since he asked which hotel I was staying at, and while I was a bit curious to learn more about him, I didn't want to risk pushing his buttons by coming off as nosey. By now, I was well aware of how easy it was to do that.

"Is this your first time in Oakland?" he asked, all of a sudden.

"Yes, but I rode through a couple times with my dad."

"So, you don't know shit about the areas then, huh..."

I paused after his weird comment. "What'chu mean by that?"

Suddenly, he took west to 880 and the Port—which was in the complete opposite direction of my hotel.

"What are you doing?" I asked, alarmed.

"Chill, I got a call from my peoples 'bout some business. This won't take long."

I couldn't recall him taking a phone call since we'd been in the hospital. All of a sudden, panic settled in and I quickly flew off the handle. "Hell no! I didn't agree to all that! You said you would take me to the hotel! You didn't say anything about making detours! You can drop me off first and *then* handle your business." I rambled anxiously.

"Or you can sit back, relax, and enjoy the ride. Stop being so muthafuckin' uptight all the time."

I relaxed a little, and tried to have faith that he wasn't *that* type of nigga. Ten minutes later, I realized my faith was unfounded. Instead of in the city, we were now in the slums, surrounded by homeless addicts and suspicious-looking characters.

"What the hell is this? And what type of business do you have to handle over here?" I asked, with a slight tremor in my voice. I could no longer mask my fear. The reality of the situation was that I was in a car with a total stranger, in a 'hood that most people avoided driving through.

"What'chu mean *over here*? You don't recognize this hood? Smart Compton girl like you?" There was a sinister grin on Q's face as he waited on a response.

"*Should* I know this hood?"

Q slowed down his speed, and I grew even more nervous. "They call this neck of the woods the Lower

Bottoms. One of the most dangerous areas in the city. Hell, even twelve don't fuck around down here. They call this the bottom of the bottom."

"Why did you bring me here?" I asked him.

"'Cuz this is where yo stop ends, if I don't get my muthafuckin' apology."

5

Q

"Pussy ain't a priority when it come to this paper."

—Q

I wasn't really gonna put her out...but I *was* gonna get a sincere apology up out that ass, but she didn't need to know all that. At this point, it wasn't even about the shirt; it was the muthafuckin' principle of the matter, and Sade needed to take accountability for her actions. "Well...I'm waiting..."

"I'm not giving you shit but a face full of mace! Now get me out of this neighborhood or I'm pepper spraying your ass!"

She went to reach for her purse, but I quickly held up the can of mace. "Lookin' for this?" I asked, waving it in her face. I'd pick-pocketed it after purposely bumping into her in the parking lot of the hospital.

Sade gasped in shock and lunged for it. "Your thieving ass! Give it back to me!" She shouted angrily.

I moved it out of her reach just in time. "You'll get it back after I get my apology."

"Q, I'm not playing with you!"

"Who the fuck said I was playing? See, that's yo muthafuckin' problem. Ain't nobody got in yo ass yet. I can tell. Now you done met the right muthafuckin' one."

"And you done met the wrong bitch! Now give me back my shit and get me the fuck up outta here!"

"You making a lot of demands for someone who's not driving. That's yo whole thing though. You think you run shit. But let me tell you something, bitch. You don't run me."

"I'm not trying to run you, Q. I just want to get back to my room." All of her false bravado melted away, and before me was a vulnerable, young woman. It damn near made my dick hard.

"I have no problem taking you back to your room...but you know what that favor requires." I stated.

Sade swallowed her pride and turned her head away. "I'm sorry I spilled your drink on you, and talked so disrespectfully. I was wrong and I acknowledge that. Now will you please take me back to the hotel?" She asked pleadingly.

Satisfied with her response, I pulled off and hopped on the freeway. "Was that so hard?" I laughed.

Sade was quiet during the entire ride. I could see the treacherous thoughts running through her mind without her even having to speak. She hated my muthafuckin' ass; it was written all over her face.

The second I pulled up to the Hilton Garden Inn, Sade snatched her seatbelt off. She was so anxious to get the fuck away from me, she almost hopped out of a moving car.

"Guess I screwed my chances of getting an invite, huh?"

Sade responded by slamming the door in my face. I figured it was a hopeless attempt, but you won't know until you shoot your shot. From the car, I watched her stomp into the hotel and then disappear inside the elevators. I couldn't even get so much as a thank you from her, but something told me I'd run into her pretty lil' ass again real soon.

***

After dropping off Sade, I decided to swing by my lil' chick Mimi's crib. I had some work stashed at her spot that I wanted to collect and take back to the city with me. Plus, I figured I could kill 2 birds with 1 stone, since it was obvious I wouldn't get none from Sade. She had me harder than a bitch, and I needed to get this nut off.

Lucky for me, Mimi was also in town for All-Star Weekend, and currently staying at her parent's vacation home in San Francisco. My product was produced in the Vrae Village of Peru, and came directly in through the Bay after clearing the border. Mimi's parent's crib was the perfect storage point, and in turn for letting me use it, I pieced her off something nice.

When I pulled into her driveway, I called Mimi to make sure she was there. Her car was parked in the driveway, but she could've easily been at a friend's house.

"Hey, baby," she answered on the 2nd ring. She was obviously waiting for a nigga to hit her line. "Where you at? I wanna see you..." She asked in her sexy ass voice.

"Good. My dick wanna see you, too. Open the door." I told her before killing the line.

Not even a minute later, Mimi appeared at the front screen in nothing but a thong. She was topless, and ready for me to bend her ass over. That was one of the reasons I fucked with Mimi. She wasn't 'bout them games. She knew what it was, and she played her role with the utmost efficiency.

Parking the car, I turned the engine off, and approached her home. When I walked inside, she grabbed my belt, ready to smash on sight. "Nigga, it took you long enough." She complained as she fumbled with my belt.

I quickly stopped her by snatching her hair. "Hold the fuck up, bitch. We got business to handle first. Pussy ain't a priority when it come to this paper." I lectured her. She wouldn't get an inch of dick until I counted the chickens and made sure every single bird was still there. I trusted Mimi, but I never put shit past anyone.

I made my way to the basement where I kept the work, and spent ten minutes making sure shit was sweet. After ensuring that things were in order, I went back upstairs and found her in the living room snorting a line. She dipped and dabbled in the nose candy, but she knew better than to offer me any. I sold coke, but I didn't use it, because it made you a liability. And in this field, there was absolutely no room for liabilities.

I could tell by Mimi's body language she had a little attitude. I didn't really give a fuck, and I still choked her bitch ass up. "Why the fuck you lookin' like that for? Huh?"

"Nigga, you know why. You had me waiting all fucking day for this dick," she purred, while unfastening my jeans. "You know how testy I get when you make me wait." she said seductively.

"Bitch, the wait gon' be worth it. That's all the fuck that matters." I said as I backed her up to the couch. Her body trembled beneath me as I kissed her neck, and made her weak in the knees. My breath on her skin had her shivering uncontrollably. She could barely contain herself.

I slipped a hand down her panties to see how ready she was.

Damn.

Her panties were soaked in her juices. "Put that dick up in me!" she bellowed. "I wanna feel you in me." She pushed her pelvis up against my erection, begging me to fuck her senseless. She had me harder than a bitch and I was definitely ready to get this nut off.

Pushing her down on the couch, I ripped her panties off, and ran my finger up and down her wet slit. She moaned and started squeezing on her breasts, grinding her pelvis against my hand.

"Fuck me, Q!" she cried out.

Grasping both of her wrists, I held them above her head and started licking and sucking on her nipples. Mimi gasped and let out a loud moan as I slipped two fingers into her slowly. I stopped sucking on her breasts, surprised at how wet and tight she was. I could feel my dick straining with anticipation, longing to be inside her.

"Quit playing with me, baby! Put it in me!" she begged.

Digging in my pocket, I tore the foil off a condom with my teeth, and rolled it down my shaft. I then slipped my fingers into her mouth, forcing her to taste her own pussy juices, and slowly I began to push my length into her. I hadn't even fully undressed. I simply pulled my jeans around my ass, too impatient to waste any more time.

"Damn," I groaned. Her pussy was so wet, I almost wanted to ditch the rubber.

Leaning forward, I spat on her clit a little, and started rubbing on it slowly. That made Mimi even wetter. She moaned and wrapped her legs around me, in an attempt to take every inch.

"You missed this dick?" I asked, wrapping a hand around her throat.

"Fuck yes, baby! You know I fucking did." She tried to thrust her hips with mine, but had a hard time keeping up with my rhythm.

Grabbing her by the waist, I held her lil' ass in place. "You ain't gotta do all that. Just lay there and take this dick. Only thing you need to be worried about is opening your mouth and saying aaaahh. You hear me, bitch?" I started pumping faster and harder. "Only thing you need to do is open wide and catch this nut!"

"SHIT, Q! YESSSSS! Yes, baby! Fuck me! Cum all in my mouth!" I made that bitch squirt, and shortly after, I felt my nut rise.

"Shit. Here it come."

Snatching off the condom, I skeeted all in her face and hair. "*Mmm.*" I grunted as I spilled my seed, letting my dick go soft in my hand.

Mimi looked disappointed after I started getting dressed. I didn't even bother to give her a washcloth to wipe the jizz out of her eyes. She probably expected this fuck-session to last well into the morning, but now that I got what I came for, I was ready to skate off with the work.

"Am I gonna see you back in the city?"

"Depends on how busy the city keeps me."

Accepting it for what it was, Mimi made the smart choice, and refrained from arguing with me. Besides, as long as she was eating, there really wasn't much to squabble over anyway. I mean, she was cool and all, and we fucked here and there, but she was nothing more than business and a nut to bust. Honestly, I didn't need another headache. My baby mama was already enough.

6

LaMar

"But you can't possibly say anything to save me from myself."

—*Camari*

Pressing a wet cloth against Camari's face, I tried to help her come down from her high. She was drunk, coked up, and unable to walk due to her ankle. To help with that, I put an ice pack on it. She was lying on the sofa in our hotel room at the Four Seasons.

"LaMar..." she mumbled. The intoxication hadn't fully kicked in until now. "Why didn't I fuck with you instead of Q?"

The question caught me off guard, and I laughed at her error. "You *did* fuck with me. You had my son, remember?"

Camari smiled drunkenly. "I don't remember that," she said.

I shook my head at her. "I meant to say you had my son aborted."

Camari stared off into the distance. "I wish I'd kept it," she confessed. "Sometimes I sit back and think about how he may've been my second chance at life. I couldn't do right by the first child...Maybe the second one would've...you know...slowed me down." Camari met my gaze calmly. There were tears in her eyes, and I could tell she was hurting inside. Knowing that she was in pain made my heart ache, too. There was so much I wanted to do for her. So much I wanted to give her...but I couldn't. She was my homie's baby mama, and the first bitch he'd ever fallen for.

At 16, me and Q were getting a lil' change, and fucking it off on stupid shit. One day, while driving along Figueroa, I jokingly offered to buy him a hooker, since the block was notorious for having them. I had no idea at the time that Q was a virgin. To make a long story short, Camari put it on that nigga, and the rest was history. Though he hated to admit it, he caught feelings for the hoe.

Little did he know, so did I. Secretly, over the course of time, I began to grow curious about her. I saw the way she had my boy sweating her, and I wanted a taste of what she was putting on him.

I fell for Camari too, and ever since a nigga just wasn't moving the same. She had my head all fucked up and she knew it. Q wasn't the only one she was hurting with this hoe shit she was on. I cared about her ass, too, so it pained me just as much to see her out there like that.

Camari was better than that, but she couldn't see it in herself. Hoeing was all that she knew. Plus, it helped feed her drug addiction. I hated to see her like this, but at 32, she was set in her ways, and not a damn thing me or Q did would change that.

"I still love you, Mar," she said, breaking into my thoughts. "You know that...right?"

"I can't tell, bitch. You still out here in these muthafuckin' streets."

"I'm only doing what I gotta do to get by. You of all people should respect that." She touched my face, and I closed my eyes, reveling in the feel of her soft fingers. I would never understand how she was capable of turning out both of our asses. Maybe it was the way she fucked. Maybe it was the way she swallowed a dick. Regardless, she had our young asses under her spell.

"Don't be like that, LaMar. You know I love you."

Taking Camari's hand, I placed a gentle kiss on the back of it. I didn't care about the meth scars around her mouth. Camari was bad as fuck to me.

At 5'6, she was midnight black with slanted hazel eyes. Other than the scars, she had nice, smooth skin, full lips, and a sexy, slim figure. The drugs and lack of self-respect equaled a pretty, evil hoe. But I was crazy about that evil hoe; she had my mind gone.

"I know you do. Sometimes love ain't enough. You taught me that shit." I ran my fingers through her hair. It was naturally long and straight. I always told her she reminded me of a chocolate Tyra Banks. "I hate to see you out here like this. If it's coke or cash you need, I can get that for you. You know me and Q knee deep in the game. You ain't gotta keep putting yourself through this. Leave that nigga Romello where he at, man. That nigga ain't on shit. It's better things out here than the shit you into."

"I love you, LaMar. I really do…Your heart is so much bigger than Q's. That's why I always fucked with you more than him. You know just what to say. You know just what a woman wants to hear," she said. "But you can't possibly say anything to save me from myself. No one can, baby." A single tear slipped from her eye, and before I could wipe it away, she placed the barrel of a gun to my throat. "Now run me dat check, dem chains, *and* the muthafuckin' keys to the 'Rarri."

7

Camari

"All these niggas were nothing but a come-up to me."

—*Camari*

Running out of the hotel, I laughed at how easy that lick was. Robbing LaMar was equivalent to taking candy from a baby. That muthafucka made this shit *too* simple for a grimey bitch like me. He was so busy pouring his heart out, he didn't notice me grabbing his gun. That pussy made nigga was food to me. I wasn't interested in shit he had to say. But I was interested in whatever was in his duffel bag. From the looks of it, that muthafucka was heavy, and from the feel of it, I assumed it was money.

Bee-lining from the establishment, I raced for his car. I hadn't twisted my ankle at all. I simply told him that shit so he'd let his guards down. I knew how soft that nigga was on me, so I figured his ass would help, and sure enough he fell for it. That soft ass nigga played right into my hand.

The performance I gave was Oscar worthy. A bitch had even shed a tear. I'd do whatever it took to secure a bag. Anybody could catch a set-up. All these niggas were nothing but a come-up to me. A meal-ticket. A pawn in my game, with Romello as the King. Looking down at the duffel bag clutched tightly in my hand, an evil grin crossed my face as I imagined how stupid LaMar must've felt. His loss would make for a great gift to Daddy. Romello loved expensive shit—especially when it belonged to his enemies.

After hitting the corner, I found his car parked along the side of the hotel. LaMar came bolting out of the building at the same time I hopped in his ride. He tried to grab the door handle but I pressed the lock button on that ass.

"You gon' have to be quicker than that," I teased as I shoved the keys into the ignition and revved the engine.

"BITCH, QUIT PLAYING AND OPEN THE MUTHAFUCKIN' DOOR!" he yelled, pounding on the window. "Get the fuck out, you schemin' ass bitch!" He banged his fist against the hood of the car. "Get the fuck out, so I can fuck you up!"

"I'm too pretty to fight! But I ain't too cute to shoot! So back the fuck up, before I let this thing go!" I said, waving the gun.

WHAM!

LaMar punched the window, cracking the glass just a little. He was just about to hit it again when I peeled off in haste. He quickly grabbed the door handle, and I dragged him for a quarter of a mile before he finally collapsed from fatigue. After leaving his ass in the dust, I headed straight for the Claremont. I couldn't wait to show Daddy what his bottom bitch had copped him.

8

LaMar

"A dog will look down when they've done wrong, but a snake will look you dead in the eyes."

—LaMar

Camari had just hit the corner when I spotted a white drop top Mustang parked at the gas station across the street. The bitch who owned it was sitting in the passenger seat with the door wide open, waiting for the fuel meter to stop running.

Rushing over before Camari got too far, I jumped in the whip, and peeled off with the nozzle still in the tank.

"HEY, WHAT THE FUCK ARE YOU DOING?!" she screamed. The bitch almost flew out the car because of how fast a nigga pulled off.

"If you don't get the fuck out this car, bitch, you gon' be hog-tied and gagged! 'Cuz that's what I do to niggas!" I threatened.

"Well, that's what you gon' have to do, 'cuz I ain't going nowhere!" she challenged.

"Suit yaself then."

Putting the pedal to the metal, I floored the accelerator in an attempt to catch up to Camari. She was going over 60 in a residential, and I prayed the bitch didn't wreck my shit. I couldn't believe this bitch had got me for over 400 G's. I couldn't let her ass get off that easy. The nigga Q would flip; after all, he was the one who had secured the deal.

"Wait...ain't you that nigga from the club earlier?" She asked with her eyes bulged out.

My thoughts were interrupted by the unexpected question. I gave her a once over, and realized that she too looked familiar. Matter fact, she was the shorty with the fatty and the stuck-up ass friend. I looked down at her thick ass thighs to make sure.

Yep, it was her. "Yeah... I am. What are the odds of us running into each?"

"Yeah, just my luck, right," she said, sarcastically.

I quickly switched the subject. "Aye, you see that car up ahead of us?" I pointed.

"The red one?" she asked, confused.

"Yeah, that's my ride," I told her. "Bitch, just hopped in my shit and skated off." I couldn't risk mentioning the money.

"Did you know the chick?"

"Something like that."

"Damn. That's fucked up. So, she set you up?"

"Yeah...guess you could say that."

"Damn, people ain't shit."

"Like the old saying goes, a dog will look down when they've done wrong, but a snake will look you dead in the eyes." That bitch Camari was foul for this shit, but I planned on making her ass suffer. And to think, I was actually in love with this hoe. Now all I wanted to do was choke the life up out her ass. Love meant nothing when you couldn't even trust a muthafucka.

"So, are you borrowing my car until you get yours back?" Jayda asked.

My attitude softened as I tried to sympathize with her. "Look, you gon' get your shit back, a'ight. Trust me. Mustangs ain't even my thing."

"Yeah, and carjacking *is*," she replied smoothly.

I gave her fine ass the side eye. She was one of the baddest bitches I'd ever seen, so I gave her ass a pass. She was cute, thick, *and* chocolate—all three of my weaknesses combined into one bad ass bitch. "Like I said, you'll get'cha shit back...I promise you, I ain't on that type of time."

"You can't even imagine the muthafuckin' night I've had! I just got out the hospital. I had to catch a cab just to pick this bitch up from the club! Then turn around and gas it up since the bitch was on E! And *then*, here you come, hopping in my shit like your ass paid for it! Just so you know, if you wreck my shit you're paying for it—"

Her rant was cut off as her body jerked forward. I had to mash my foot down hard on the breaks in order to avoid a nasty collision. Camari had just run the red light at the intersection with her middle finger up in the air. I was on my way to do the same before a pickup came careening towards me blaring its horn.

By the time that muthafucka passed me by, Camari was already gone, leaving a cloud of exhaust and dust in her wake. My money, jewelry, and Ferrari were now far beyond my grasp. "FUCK! FUCK! FUCK!" I screamed, punching the steering wheel over and over again.

"Aye, chill! What the fuck are you doing?! Didn't I just tell your ass that this is a rental?!"

"Bitch, fuck yo rental and fuck you! Bum ass bitch!"

Hopping out her ride, I dug in my sock for the spare change I kept on me, and threw it at her. Camari had no idea about that secret stash. It was $600, and all I had left to my name, but it was more than enough to compensate for the inconvenience I'd caused.

"Fuck you, too!" Burning rubber, Jayda peeled off, leaving me in a gust of smoke.

Now I had to think up a damn good lie to tell Q.

I guess this was what I get for fucking on his baby momma to begin with. Like they say, karma's a bitch.

9

Camari

"Am I gon' have to put a bullet in yo ass to get my point across?"

—*Romello*

After copping some yams on LaMar's dime, I got high in his car in an alley not far from Romello's hotel. The initial plan was to bring *everything* to him, but I couldn't resist spending some of the money that was burning a hole in my pocket. I couldn't believe I came up on so much cash, but LaMar did say they were knee deep in the game.

Gone off the lick I hit, I indulged myself in the drugs. I refused to share them with my wives, because they were always smoking up my shit.

Naytoma and Chelsie weren't really my wives but I called them that because we all shared the same pimp. Hoeing for him was equivalent to a marital commitment.

We all lived together. We all worked the Blade for him, and we all brought the paper home to Daddy. I loved my wives as if we'd taken actual vows, but I swear them hoes could make me sick.

Apart from smoking up my drugs, they were always wearing my clothes and borrowing shit without my permission. But I guess no one said marriage was easy. Still, they were my family, and all that I knew and lived for.

When Romello snatched my ass off Figg, I was at my lowest point in life. Homeless, broke, and fucking for pocket change. Regardless of my circumstances, Romello saw the potential in me. He came and changed a real hoe and the rest was history.

After getting my fill of crack-cocaine, I finally made my way back to Daddy so he could see what all I'd copped him. Dropping the car at valet, I made my way up to his suite and found Naytoma and Chelsie cooking breakfast naked. It was a quarter after 9 a.m., and I hadn't realized until now how long I'd been gone. When you were high, it was easy to lose track of the time.

"Welcome back, baby mama. We missed you," Naytoma greeted.

My wives may have been white, but they were built like some sistas, and they were experts at breaking bread. We made so much money for Romello, that he could've easily gotten my teeth fixed, but he claimed I sucked dick better without 'em. A couple years ago, he knocked two of them out the one time I got out of line. I never tried his ass again after that shit.

At 29, Chelsie was a vet like me. She was ¼th Puerto Rican, so she had that light skinned mixed look the niggas loved. She had dark brunette hair and a slim thick build. I called her ass the million-dollar mouth because of her finesse. She could talk a nigga out his pockets in a matter of seconds.

Both women were whipping up something that smelled nice, and I couldn't have been happier. My high had worn off, and a bitch was hungrier than a muthafucka.

"Welcome back my ass. Where the fuck you been at all night?" Romello was seated at the wet bar, rolling a blunt laced with cocaine. He smoked them shits like they were going out of style, but I was the *last* bitch to judge. "You gon' make me ask again bitch," he said, when I didn't respond quick enough. "Don't make me get the fuck up out this chair."

"Relax, baby. I been making plays."

"*Relax*?? Bitch, who the fuck is you talking to?!" Snatching his gat off the countertop, he climbed off the barstool and got up in my face. "Hoe, I'll blow a hole through yo muthafuckin' head! I own you, bitch! Not the other way around! You bring yo black ass to me before you make any type of play! I need to know where this pussy is at all muthafuckin' times!" He said one thing, but I knew truthfully, he didn't want me holding out on him. He thought I would bust a lick and not give him his percentage. And although, I might shave a little off top, I would never take the whole cut for myself.

Suddenly, Romello shoved his gun in my face. "Bitch, do you hear me talking to you? Or am I gon' have to put a bullet in yo ass to get my point across???"

Turned on by his overly aggressive behavior, I started sucking the barrel of the pistol like a dick. Romello thought his threats would frighten me, but all it did was make my pussy wet.

"*Mmm.* I think I do need something in my ass." I ran my tongue along the cold metal like I was licking the shaft of a penis.

"Bitch, you better quit playing with me, 'fore I put this hammer on yo ass. Now what the fuck you got...besides all this," he asked, squeezing on my booty. "You claim you been making plays all night, so I know you got that bag for a nigga."

"Baby, I got the bag, the bread, *and* a brand new Rarri for you," I cheesed, handing him the duffel bag and keys.

Romello peeked inside the duffel bag and a smile spread across his face. He already knew that it belonged to LaMar because it was the same bag he hit him with in the club. "You the best hoe that ever lived," he said, kissing me.

"You my muthafuckin' Daddy. How else am I supposed to be? You the best thing in my life. I gotta go hard. I'm on your team, baby. Always. Now take this money to kick off your rap career. You deserve it."

Pulling me closer, he kissed me again. "This is really forever. Understand me?"

"Yes, baby. I know it is." And I wasn't just gassing him like I did most of these tricks. I meant every single word of it. Romello was my beginning, my middle, and my end.

10

Sade

"I can't blame the nigga for getting your ass together."

—*Jayda*

When I awoke the following morning, I was surprised to find Jayda in the bed next to me. I expected her to spend the night with Romello, but from the look of things, there'd been a change of plans. Grabbing a pillow, I launched it at her head. "Wake up, hoe!"

"What happened?? What is it??" Jayda quickly jerked her head up alarmed, but relaxed when she saw that it was me.

"When the fuck did your ass get back here? I ain't hear you creeping in last night."

"Bitch, you won't believe the crazy ass shit that happened after I left the hospital! So, you remember that fool you bumped into at the club?"

I rolled my eyes. "How could I forget?" Q made it hard for me to forget anything about him and the interesting night we shared.

"Bitch, tell me why his nigga jacked my ride last night!"

My eyes shot open at that shocking bit of news. "BITCH, WHAT! On God???"

"Bitch, on god, he did! The nigga jumped right in my shit at the gas station, and sped the fuck off! I almost flew out that bitch 'cuz the door was wide open! He was chasing some bitch that robbed him. Apparently, she ran off with the nigga's ride, so he jacked my shit to chase her down in."

"What the fuck, Jayda, are you serious?" First, she gets shot in a nightclub, then she gets carjacked following her release from the hospital. I swear this bitch had the worst luck in Oakland, and I for one, couldn't wait to get out of this damn city before it rubbed off on me.

"Girl, I *wish* I was playing," she said.

"Oh my god, Jayda. That shit is fucking crazy." I quickly climbed off my bed and sat on hers, as if being closer would somehow console her. Her night was definitely crazier than mine. "I can't believe that happened to you. That's some wild ass shit. How did you get the car back—*Did* you get it back???"

"Hell yeah! He never caught up with the hoe. He had no choice but to give me back my shit if he ain't want me to put your daddy on his ass," she laughed. "'Cuz you know I would've. And I know what they do to pretty boys like him in the pen."

"So now he's pretty?"

"I swear, if he hadn't jacked my ride, he probably would've gotten this ass. On me, that nigga was so fine he had my muthafuckin' panties wet that whole time. And not only was he bae, the nigga paid me for all the hassle. Look." Jayda dug in her bra and pulled out 6 crisp Franks.

"He gave that to you???" I asked, grabbing for the money. "You sure *you* weren't the one who robbed him?" I had to touch it just to make sure that it was real.

Jayda quickly moved it out of reach. "Nah, my bitch. I said he gave it to *me*! Not you!"

"Well, you know sharing is caring."

"Bitch, you wanna share something? Share the details from last night! What the fuck went down with you and Q? Did he give you a *ride* or nah???" she laughed, humping her pillow.

I grabbed the pillow and hit her with it, fucking up her hair.

"Bitch, do *not* play! It wasn't even like that! He only took me to the hospital and then back to the room." I paused. "Well...he did make a quick detour—"

"To where? His bedroom?" she laughed.

"Bitch, I told you it wasn't even like that! He literally drove me to these slums called the Lower Bottoms. Then he threatened to leave me stranded if I didn't apologize."

"Did you?"

I rolled my eyes at her. "Bitch, what do you think?"

"Damn," she giggled. "That muthafucka is savage. But, bitch, you did have that shit coming. I can't blame the nigga for getting your ass together," she said.

"Whatever. To hell with that nigga. I'm just glad I don't have to see his ass again." Little did I know, at the time, how wrong I was.

11

Q

"She was still my responsibility, whether she wanted to be or not."

—Q

The sun was just beginning to rise, and a muthafucka was finally on his way back to the telly for a shower and a quick power nap before I got back on the road. Nigga had been in the streets all night, making plays for the last few hours. All-Star Weekend wasn't the only reason that brought me out to Oakland. I was here for business just as much as I was pleasure.

Me and LaMar had the streets on lock in all parts of Cali. Muthafucka had to get it. Bills were due soon, and my son's birthday was in just a few weeks. I had to collect, and make these moves in order to keep shit in rotation. It was my responsibility to make sure everyone around me continued eating.

After arriving at the Four Seasons, I pulled up to valet and was just about to hop out when I noticed a phone lying in the passenger's seat. Upon further investigation, I realized it belonged to Sade. The bitch was so pressed to get up to her room, she fucked around and left her brick in my ride. Grabbing the Nokia, I shoved it in my back pocket and headed up to the 30th floor.

When I opened the door to my penthouse suite, I expected to find Camari but was instead greeted by silence. The place was completely empty.

Where the fuck did this bitch wander off to now?

Camari could be such a pain in my ass, but she was my responsibility, whether she wanted to be or not. My feelings for her might've wavered over the years, but the fact of the matter remained the same; she was the mother of my son, and once the love of my life. We might not have saw eye to eye, but I cared about her tremendously, and never wanted to see her hurt.

Feeling obligated to check on Camari, I called her phone and was sent straight to voicemail. I then hit up LaMar, but his ass wasn't picking up either.

"Man, what kinda bullshit is they on?" I asked the empty hotel suite.

Usually, LaMar made rounds with me, but I'd stuck him with the task of watching Camari. Now they both weren't answering my calls. LaMar was a night owl and Camari's crackhead ass never slept, so shit just wasn't adding up. Something was fishy, but I couldn't quite call it...

Pushing those worries to the back of my mind, I pulled Sade's phone out and looked at it. I wondered how long it'd be until she realized it was gone. She didn't seem that intuitive since her ass was always running her mouth. Something told me her ass was a handful. But I didn't give a fuck, I was still on her head, and when it was said and done, I planned on making her ass mine.

12

LaMar

"Man, we in these streets hard-bodied."

—*Q*

I swear I walked the block for hours before I finally took my ass back to the hotel. Needless to say, I was madder than a muthafucka about my ride, money, and jewelry being taken. Nigga like me never got caught slipping, and here it was, I let a piece of pussy get over on me. If my soldiers found out about this shit, they'd lose all respect for me. Hell, I barely could even look at myself.

After hours of aimless walking, I finally made my way up to my penthouse, where Q was inside waiting on me. He had his phone to his ear when I walked in, but quickly hung up the moment he saw me. I presumed he was calling my phone, but that muthafucka had died hours ago.

"Fuck is going on?" Q asked, with a hint of irritation in his tone.

Judging from his body language, I couldn't tell if he knew what happened with Camari. Just thinking about the shit had me ready to put hands and feet on that bitch. On top of that, him not seeing my car would have me looking extra sus, but what the fuck was I gonna tell him? *Yo bro, your baby momma robbed me*? Shit didn't even sound right. In fact, I was only supposed to take Camari back to his room. I never bargained for any of this shit happening. I would've never had a bitch around me I thought was capable of robbing me. I trusted the hoe. But that's where I made the mistake. Too bad her dumb ass was gonna have to the learn the hard way that I'm not one to be fucked with.

"Well? Where the fuck is Camari?" Q asked, snapping me out of my thoughts.

Judging from the scowl on this nigga face, I knew that he was pissed off.

"Wus good, nigga," I greeted, giving him a pound.

"Fuck you mean wus good? A nigga been calling you since I dropped shorty off. Then, I called Camari's hoe ass and she sent my shit straight to voicemail three times," Q said, sounding irritated.

"My fault, bro. Nigga got caught up in some bullshit."

"Like what?"

"Man, you ain't gon' believe this shit, but I dropped the bitch Camari off—"

"I thought I told you to bring her straight to the hotel."

"Lemme finish the story, man. You gon' be happy that hoe ain't here, 'cuz if she was you would kill this bitch. Anyways, I dropped the bitch off, and the hoe got out the car walking regular as fuck," I said. "Bitch straight gamed us with that fake ass twisted ankle act."

"Nigga, you bullshittin'," Q said in disbelief. I already knew he was over Camari's bullshit, but this shit just made it worse. "On God, I'm done with her hoe ass."

Little did he know, I felt the same fucking way.

"Fuck her then. Not my monkey, not my circus. Anyway, check out's in a couple hours. I'mma get a quick nap in, then we headed back to the city. I think I tied up all loose ends here."

I scratched behind my ear and looked away, a clear indication that I was getting ready to lie. "Oh. Um...about that..." I began. "I haven't finished telling you the rest of the story. So, as I'm dropping Camari off, a couple niggas from Romello's camp come out of nowhere and jugged me," I lied. "I think she set that shit up, too." I said, adding extra flair to my lie. "Them muthafuckas took me for everything I had!"

"Fuck you mean they took you for everything??? Where the fuck is the muthafuckin' money????" he yelled, looking around frantically.

"I just told you they took it, man. And every muthafuckin' thing else I had on me." I patted my empty chest. I usually wore a Jesus piece, but Camari snatched that too. And what's sad is the bitch ain't have a drop of faith in her DNA. "They got everything, homie. My chains, my watch, my car—"

"Nigga, fuck yo chains and watch! That was close to half a mil! How the fuck you let this shit happen?!"

"Man, I got'chu—"

"Man, we in these streets hard-bodied! Nigga, you know what type of enemies we got! You know how this shit go! Man, how the fuck could you get caught slipping?" He fired off at me, only making me feel lower.

"When I say I got'chu, I got'chu, big homie. I know. I fucked up big time. But don't worry, my nigga. When I catch homie, shots gon' go. I'm playing target practice with that nigga's head. On God, I'mma get our shit back, and we gon' keep this shit in rotation."

13

Sade

"A bitch was tired of struggling to make ends meet."

—*Sade*

"Jayda, have you seen my phone?" I asked, after grabbing my suitcase off the luggage carousel. We'd just touched down at LAX when I suddenly realized I didn't have it. Initially, I assumed it was in one of my bags, but now I was positive that I'd either lost or misplaced it.

"No, babes. I didn't see it. You want me to call it," she offered.

"Please," I said, patting my pockets for what felt like the hundredth time.

"I'm calling it but it's steadily going to voicemail," she told me.

I sighed in frustration. "That means it's dead."

"Chill. It may be in one of ya bags."

"Damn. I hope so," I said, following her out of the airport.

After hailing a cab, I climbed in and searched aimlessly for my device. It wasn't like me to be irresponsible. I didn't drink or smoke, so I was usually on my shit. I guess with everything that'd happened last night, I had somehow lost track of it.

Maybe it's buried deep in my luggage, I told myself. *Hopefully I'll find it once we get back home.*

Pushing those worries to the back of my mind, I relaxed and took in the scenery as we headed back to the home we shared in Carson. During the entire trip, I found myself thinking and fantasizing about Q.

A smile tugged at my lips as my mind wandered endlessly. Something about Q made me drawn to him, despite our rough introduction. Not only was the nigga sexy, he had a swag that was out of this world. As angry as he'd made me, I kinda liked the way he bossed up on me.

As the youngest, I'd been spoiled most of my life, and had a bad habit of treating people fucked up—even the ones I considered closest. No one had ever really checked me about it until Q. And while I loathed his approach at making me realize this, I also sort of respected it.

Damn him for getting in my head, I cursed.

I had sworn that I'd left my feelings for him in Oakland, but they somehow still lingered about.

Damn him straight to hell, right along with that damn jersey.

Suddenly, the foul stench of rotting meat slapped me in the face. We were passing Miracle Market, the spot most people in the hood brought their poultry and beef. Right across the street were The Forms, a ran down community that was known for sheltering drug addicts. Crack coupled with the stench of rotting meat was an instant reminder that I needed to get the fuck out of Compton. Sure, it was my home, but there was so much out there other than pawn shops, liquor stores, burger stands, and gang bangers.

I prayed that my career took me to higher levels. Jayda and I were both freelance photographers but neither one of us were making enough to sustain on our own, which was why we chose to be roomies. We could've just as easily moved back in with our parents, but who the hell wanted that life?

Something had to give.

A bitch was tired of struggling to make ends meet.

I shook my head in disappointment at a stop sign riddled with bullets. It was right across the street from *King Drew Medical Center*, which was also called Killer King. It got the nickname because of its poor health services, and the fact that it was the only hospital in the area. Anyone that got shot in Compton, Watts or any other surrounding area had to go to that hospital, and the chances of survival were always slim. I knew that firsthand, because it was where my mom had died.

Passing Compton, the taxi driver took Central Avenue all the way down to Carson. Back in the day, the neighborhood used to be filled with whites until the poverty-stricken came in and took over. Separated from Compton by the 91 Freeway, Carson was a city known for its high crime and huge Crips population. Luckily, me and my girl hadn't experienced any problems, but if ever we did, my dad was just a phone call away.

"Home sweet home," Jayda sang, as we pulled into our driveway.

The taxi driver helped us unload our suitcases and I graciously tipped him $20, even though Jayda's ass clearly had more cash. After the cabbie pulled off, we lugged our bags to the door. Jayda was just about to stick the key in when we heard the unmistakable sound of a milli cocking behind us.

"Run me yo shit, bitch!"

14

Sade

"I don't claim the streets. The streets claim me."

—*Shadow*

The hairs stood on the nape of my neck as I felt the cold metal press into me. Regardless of the compromising situation I was in, I still reached for my purse for my can of mace.

"Chill out, sis, I'm just fucking with you," Shadow laughed.

I turned around and punched the shit out of my brother's chest. "Boy, why the fuck you play so damn much?! You scared the shit out of me!"

Jayda exhaled at the same time that I did. We were both pretty shook.

Sharif, known in the streets as Shadow, was my older brother. The nigga was always in and out of jail, and a known jack boy in the streets. My father had pretty much disowned him after finding out about his gang affiliation. Come to think of it, they'd always bumped heads throughout his life, but it only seemed to worsen after mom's death. After she passed, our entire family fell apart. Shadow really started wildin out, and my father couldn't control him. I don't think there was any saving their relationship at this point.

"You know a nigga couldn't resist!" he laughed. "On mud, ya'll make shit too easy!"

"Nigga, when the fuck did you get out???" Jayda questioned, with hands on hips.

"Just this morning," he said. "Shit, I was at my folk's crib up in SP, waiting on ya'll muthafuckas to land."

SP, or Stevenson Park, was known Crip territory in Carson, and there was always some shit popping off—that almost always involved Shadow. I'd told his ass way too many times to stop kicking it in them projects, but it was obvious that he was going to do whatever the fuck he wanted to do. Speaking of Crip, he was repping his colors in a blue jersey, baggy shorts, and blue snap back.

At 23, Shadow was a spitting image of our father with his dark cocoa skin, piercing light brown eyes, and dimpled chin. He had the words *Nutty Blocc Mob* tatted on his forearm, *I Hate Jesus* written across his throat, and the letters *IC* stamped below his right eye. There was a 6-inch scar on the top of his head, from where his shit was split open by a rival gang member. The hair never grew over the scar, and it was always visible.

Shadow was a proud member of the Insane Crips, the largest African-American criminal street gang on the East Side of Long Beach, California. Them niggas were some wild ass killas. Shadow started running with them after he got locked up in Long Beach, and ever since, that's who he repped.

"So, how was Oakland?" he asked, peeping our suitcases. "Heard ya'll was out there kicking it with all dem slob ass niggas."

"Fuck what you heard, nigga! Put that blower away and help us with these muthafuckin' bags," Jayda demanded. Unlike most people, she wasn't afraid of my brother or his dangerous reputation.

To everyone else, he was a savage, but to Jayda, he was like her big brother. She'd been knowing me so long, that she sorta adopted him as her own sibling, and he got on her nerves just as much as he got on mine. Tucking away his pistol, Shadow helped us inside with our bags. Afterwards, he grabbed a beer from the fridge, and made himself comfortable on the couch.

"So...how's everything been, Shadow?" Jayda asked.

He shrugged and took a swig from the bottle. "Shit. Out'chea keeping it solid in the streets. You know...same ole' same ole'."

"You ain't lying about that." I frowned in disgust as he propped his dirty ass feet on my cream throw pillow. He was still wearing his shower shoes from the County jail. Some things never did change. "Now that's some nut ass institutionalized shit! Why the hell wouldn't you throw them nasty things away?" I asked, slapping his feet off the sofa. Getting fucking prison germs all over my furniture.

"Aye, what can I say? I'mma different type of animal. Ya feel me."

"No, nigga, I don't. Now get your ass up and let's go! I'm taking you to Vintage Kicks."

"Fallback, small back. I don't need you to take me nowhere." He was always calling me small back because I had no booty, I hated that shit. "Trust me. My name good out here. Fuck I look like letting my lil' sister drop paper on me? I'mma grown ass nigga, in case you ain't get the memo," he laughed. "I got all angles covered when it come to this paper."

My eyes grew big as he pulled out a fat wad of cash. "What the hell, Sharif? Where did you get all that money?"

"You don't need all the details. Just know I'm doing what I do. A muthafucka trying to swim out here. I ain't trying to fuck around and sink."

"Nigga, you ain't even been home a whole twenty-four hours, and you already busting licks?? Are you stupid or something? Do you wanna go back to jail?" I hit him upside his head to knock some sense into him, because that was definitely where he was headed—if he didn't end up in a box first.

"Fuck you mean? Nigga gotta eat. I ain't trying to go hungry. I'm trying to get this muthafuckin' money. We in these streets."

"Aight, you keep fucking around, and your black ass gon' be back in jail. Look, Sharif, you're my big brother. The only brother that I have. I don't want to see you end up down that road again."

"And I won't. Trust me. I'm good out here."

"And how do you know that? 'Cuz you *claim* the streets got your back?"

"I don't claim the streets. The streets claim me."

"Whatever, Sharif. Just promise me, you'll stay your ass outta trouble."

"Now you know a nigga can't do that—"

"Sharif—"

"Look, I'mma go catch something tonight, then after this lick, a nigga gon' slow down. We pull this off, we gon' be set. That much I can guarantee."

I wasn't sure who he planned to rob tonight. I only prayed this wasn't his last lick. Lord knows, Shadow had a habit of gambling with his own life. I had a strong feeling that one day he was going to pick the wrong enemy.

***

After my brother left, I looked all through my luggage one last time before determining that I lost my phone somewhere between a nightclub brawl, and almost being stranded by a complete stranger. I'd just gotten back from the Sprint store and was setting up a new one when I heard a knock at the front door.

Setting my phone down, I went to open it thinking Jayda forgot something, since she left to go grocery shopping not too long ago. "Damn bitch, I'm coming," I hollered as I snatched the door open without checking the peephole.

"Hey baby." My ex-boyfriend, Frederick, greeted me, like we were still rocking like that.

"Freddy what are you doing here?" I asked him as I folded my arms and frowned my face up.

"I knew you were back in town, so I came to see you. Plus, I heard about the shootout at some nightclub and wanted to make sure you were good," he said as he wrinkled his nose up in disgust.

Freddy was so damn stuck up that I was surprised he could walk with that stick in his ass. Our whole relationship he was always critiquing me, or telling me how to talk, or how to dress, or how to act. He thought just because his family had a little money that he could tell me what the fuck to do.

I mean, yeah, I grew up in a two-parent household, for the most part and my daddy was a cop, but I still had a little hood in me. And that drove Freddy and my daddy crazy. "Well, I'm fine, as you can see, so goodbye." I said as I tried to shut the door on him.

"Sade, don't be like that," he said, grabbing the door and rudely pushing past me into my apartment. "Why are you ignoring my calls? I thought we were good?" He pleaded.

"No, you thought you could run me," I said, jabbing my finger into his chest.

"That's yo whole thing though. You think you run shit. But let me tell you something, bitch. You don't run me."

Q's words suddenly ran through my mind and Frederick's begging ass seemed even less appealing than before. Despite the fact that he was tall, dark, and handsome Freddy's personality made him so ugly. He resembled a young Morris Chestnut with more hair, but that didn't change the fact that he was a pompous ass.

"I don't think I run you, I just know what's best for you," he stated condescendingly.

"Same fucking difference nigga!" I yelled back at him.

"See, that's what I'm talking about. You're so beautiful, but you talk like gutter trash," he spat at me.

"And you are so fucking delusional," I said as I pinched the bridge of my nose and shook my head. "I don't need you to tell me what's best for me, okay? I can figure that out on my own," I told him.

"But Sade, with a little polishing, you would be perfect. And with my family's law firm, and your father's connections, nothing could stop us," he said trying to make his case.

"Oh my god!" I shouted in exasperation. "You don't respect my art, you don't respect my choices, you don't even respect me as a person. Can you just leave already?" I asked, getting angrier by the minute.

Just then, Jayda came bursting through the door. "What's all that fucking shouting in here?" she asked as she dropped the bags with the groceries by the front door.

"Everything is cool, Jayda. Freddy was just leaving, weren't you?" I said smugly as I placed my left hand on my hip and gestured toward the open door with my right.

"Right...," he said after pausing and giving me a death stare. "It just got ghetto in here anyway," he said looking Jayda squarely in the face on his way out.

"You ol' bougie wanna be Morris Chestnut nigga with a fucked-up line-up!" Jayda yelled after him. Freddy turned to argue with her, like the bitch ass nigga he was, but Jayda slammed the door in his face. "Can't stand that proper ass nigga," she said as she picked up the groceries and carried them to the kitchen. Jayda and Freddie hated each other and never missed an opportunity to try and belittle each other. "I don't even know what you saw in that stuffy ass nigga, anyway, prolly can't even fuck right," Jayda said dismissively.

"Sure can't," I said giving a nervous chuckle.

15

Shadow

"Trust me, we gon' burn all them niggas!"

—*Shadow*

A few hours later and a few homies deep, I sat parked in a light blue Plymouth Voyager on 126th street in Compton. Me and my young boys were gripping, on some get down or lay down type of shit. Tupac's *"Hit Em Up"* poured through the custom speakers as I filled my lungs with the finest kush Cali had to offer. Since I'd just gotten home from a 7-month bid, I was smoking that shit like it was wrapped in gold. Me and my main hittaz were in Piru territory, but ask any of us if we gave a fuck. We were running down on niggas, and we ain't give a damn what set they claimed. Nobody's trap was safe in the hood.

"Aye, cuz. There go them slob ass nigga right there," Dreeco pointed out. After licking his fingers clean, he wiped his hands, and grabbed his automatic. He had the whole muthafuckin' van smelling like Louisiana Fried Chicken. We'd stopped at the one on Alondra Blvd. prior to coming here. "Look like them niggas got that white girl with 'em, too. Just like you said." The overwhelming excitement in his voice couldn't be contained. We made our living off running up in traps, stealing the work, and selling it at street value. Now that I was out the joint, I planned to have the block back in motion.

Dreeco cocked his gun, and my hittaz followed suit. They were anxious to put something hot in these niggas. All I had to do was say the word, and it'd be lights out for them niggas. I swear, all my colleagues were some savages, just like me.

"Now c'mon, cuz. You know a nigga keep his ear to the streets. Not even jail could change that shit. Hell, if anything, it only made me *more* informed. Shit, you know how niggas love to talk. That's an easy call," I told them.

Plus, we weren't the only enemies them stunting hoe ass niggas had made. There was a long list of people that wanted to see 'em knocked off top, including myself. Parked directly across the street from their trap, we watched as Q and LaMar made their final drop-off. I'd been watching and studying them niggas a while now, so I had their routine down pact. They were supposed to be some high-level kingpins, but they had no idea they were being plotted on. Unfortunately, they weren't moving as militant as they thought they were, and that's where they fucked up.

"Aye, fam, careful of the police," my homie said as 12 drove by.

There was no doubt in my mind that they were on Q's payroll, and making rounds to ensure there were no interceptions. He and LaMar might've been two deep, but them niggas always had some form of protection. I knew because I'd been trying to rob these niggas for the past 2 years. But getting to them wasn't as easy as it seemed. They weren't stupid and they damn sure weren't blind to the fact that they had enemies.

"Niggas be on some funny shit. These muthafuckas really got off-duty cops on they payroll?" I laughed.

"Man, fuck them fag ass pigs, cuz. We up next! Fuck the muthafuckas that's behind us! Twelve can't stop what we got planned for these niggas! We gon' run drills on these niggas till they all drop!"

After the cops bent the corner, I decided it was time to make our move. They would have to pass 3 lights to round the block again, and if we acted fast enough, we could be in and out before their final round.

"A'ight, we finna get at these niggas," I said, grabbing my gat. I planned on putting a bullet in them niggas' heads and taking every brick they had for myself. Them muthafuckas might've thought they were the kings of Cali, but I planned on taking they crowns, coke, and whatever the fuck else I felt was worth claiming.

Hopping out the van, we snuck up on them as they headed to their cars. They were shooting the shits with each other and completely unaware of our presence. Separated by a tall fence around the apartment their trap was in, we were easily able to stay hidden in the shadows.

Q was just about to hop in his Viper, when I ran up on his turf and started dumping.

"PUSSY FUCK NIGGA!"

POP!

POP!

POP!

Glass shattered as I shot his window out. Staggering to the ground, he reached for his waist and fired back.

POP!

POP!

My hittaz started busting at LaMar, who took shelter behind his Honda S2000.

Tat! Tat! Tat! Tat! Tat! Tat! Tat! Tat!

Dreeco sprayed up the whip with his semi-automatic, taking out the tires and all four windows. Since they seemed to have shit on lock outside, I decided to run up in the trap and take the work, but before I could even kick the door in, a sea of red niggas rushed out and started shooting at us.

POP!

POP!

POP!

POP!

Ducking for cover, I missed a bullet to the face by a mere few seconds, but one still managed to clip the side of my right arm and leg. After changing my magazine, I raised my hand and fired back at them niggas, releasing uncoordinated shots that hit everything but my intended targets. Due to the fact that I was on the ground, I couldn't really see where they were at or where they were coming from. All I knew was that I couldn't let them take me out. I'd made a promise to baby sis. A promise that I wouldn't let this lifestyle be the death of me, and right now it seemed like I was falling short.

POP!

POP!

POP!

POP!

POP!

POP!

We banged it out right there in the projects, until more niggas in red came out shooting. Accepting the fact that we were easily outnumbered, we retreated with one of my niggas taking a bullet to the back of the head. I quickly jumped in the van just as the front window was shot out.

KSSSSSHHHH!

Glass shattered and sprayed everywhere, damn near getting into my eyes. Dreeco and the rest of my hittaz hopped in, throwing gang signs out the window as we skirted off. Dreeco let off a few more shots for the fuck of it.

Tat! Tat! Tat! Tat! Tat! Tat! Tat! Tat!

He didn't land any of them, and it was sad to say this entire shit was a bust. I never expected all them niggas would be crammed in that tiny ass trap, or that they'd be packing heavy artillery. I guess that's why they say looks could be deceiving.

"Man, what the fuck, man?! Them niggas killed Dartaveon!" Dreeco yelled, heated. Dartaveon was his younger cousin, so he was understandably pissed off about that shit. "Aye, homie, I need that fade! I need that fade from every single one of them niggas, man! Turn this bitch around, nigga, it ain't over!"

"Nigga, it's over. You ain't see all them niggas out there!" I hollered. "Look, I know you pissed off! You got every muthafuckin' right to be, but you gotta keep yo emotions in check, homie! You acting on emotions, instead of logic will get you killed! Trust me, we gon' burn all them niggas! We gon' clean these niggas out and get these niggas out the way!" I'd underestimated Q, but I promised myself I wouldn't make that fatal mistake again. "That muthafucka better keep his head on swivel."

16

Jayda

"He was the reason I loved crazy ass, gang-banging street niggas."

—*Jayda*

I was up, reading the *Coldest Winter Ever* when I heard a light tap on my window. My first thought was to grab the bat beside my bed, but I relaxed when I noticed it was Shadow. *What the hell is this fool on*, I asked myself. He'd startled the shit out of me, because I was so engrossed in this good ass book.

Climbing off my bed, I walked over towards the window, and slid it up as far as it could go. The lever at the top was broken, so it wouldn't open very far. "Shadow, what the fuck are you doing?"

"Waiting on you to open the damn door," he said with an attitude.

"Alright, alright. Don't get your boxers in a bunch. Here I come." After sliding my feet into a pair of slippers, I headed to the front of the house and opened the door for him—

"Shadow, oh my God! What the hell happened to you?!" I started freaking out once I saw all the blood.

"Chill. It's nothing," he said, stumbling inside. "Where's Sade?"

"Fool, sleeping! Like everyone else at this hour. Now are you gonna tell me what happened or not?"

Instead of answering my question, he took me by the hand and led me to my bedroom. Closing the door quietly behind him, he proceeded to remove his bloodstained clothes. "I need to use the shower and clean these cuts," he said.

I found that somewhat odd, considering that he lived with his on again off again girlfriend, Tia, but perhaps there was trouble on the home front.

"You couldn't have taken a shower and cleaned your cuts at Tia's?"

"Me and that bitch ain't rockin' like that," he simply said.

"Well, what about your homeboys?"

"Man, I could. But shit hot right now," he said, with a hint of agitation in his tone. He was starting to become annoyed with all of my questions.

I wanted to ask him about his injuries, but I knew that would be pushing it. Once he pulled his shirt off, I realized they weren't as severe as I'd thought. Knowing Shadow, he'd probably gotten himself into some shit. His ass was always into something. He was a street nigga, and prone to danger, but it was those very things that attracted me to him.

Taking a seat on the edge of my bed, I admired his chocolate skin and muscular build. That muthafucka was blacker than 12 a.m., and fine as all fuck. Tall, lean, and slightly bow-legged, he was a work of art, and beyond well-endowed. My pussy started throbbing as I eyed the bulge in the center of his briefs. The nigga was packing heat. He had to be at least 12 inches.

Suddenly, Shadow noticed me watching him from the corner of his eye. "You looking like you want something..."

There was dried blood all over his chiseled body, but the sight of him still made my clit tingle. "I want you to get your dirty ass in the shower," I laughed, hiding my obvious attraction.

Shadow slowly made his way towards my bed. "Nah, bitch, yo ass want something else..."

Before I could lie a second time, he grabbed me by the neck, kissed me hard, and then slapped my cheek. "I see you still out here fucking with these fuck niggas."

I rubbed my stinging cheek. "What'chu mean?"

"Bitch, don't act dumb. I know you ran yo hoe ass to Oakland for that wanna-be slob ass rapper! Lemme find out you giving away my pussy, I'mma fuck yo fucking ass up! You hear me?"

Honestly, the only reason I liked Romello was because he reminded me of Shadow. They even kinda favored each other. Whenever Shadow was in jail, I found myself lusting after the closest thing to him—and for now, that was Romello.

"Nigga, you were fucking off with Tia last time I checked. Plus, your ass was locked up, so you had no ownership over this pussy."

Snatching me up by my hair, Shadow placed his gun to my head. "I don't give a fuck who I'm with, or where I'm at. Bitch, I own this pussy. And don't you ever fucking forget it."

"Get that fucking gun out my face, Shadow, and keep your damn voice down," I hissed. "What if Sade hears us!"

Sade had no idea that me and her brother had been fucking around behind her back for years. I could only imagine her disappointment if she ever found out, and honestly, I never intended for her to.

Shadow had taken my virginity at the age of 16. He gave me my first real taste of the dark side. He was the reason I loved crazy ass, gang-banging street niggas.

"I'm serious, Sharif! Get that shit out my face!" I said, smacking the gun away. On the low, his lunatic ways turned me on, our relationship was beyond dysfunctional, but it was all that I knew.

"Shut the fuck up, bitch. I'll put this gun in yo pussy if I want," he threatened.

"No the fuck you won't. That's your problem. Your ass is outta control. You need a bitch to put you back in your place."

"And you that bitch?" Pushing me onto the bed, Sharif spread my thighs and then lowered himself at my waist. "How many times I gotta tell you, you can't tame no street nigga." I gasped in surprise as he pulled my labia open, and pressed cool steel against my clit. The overwhelming sensation sent chills down my spine and made my toes curl. I thought about asking if it was loaded, but the shit felt so good I didn't give a fuck.

Arching my back, I enjoyed the sensation of him rubbing the tip of his Glock against my pussy. He leaned in just a few inches away from my clit, and lightly blew on it, making me shiver all over.

"Who pussy is this?" he asked.

I rubbed and pinched my nipples as I told him it was his. Shadow bit the inside of my thigh, causing my hips to buck forward at his delicate teasing. He wrapped his arms around my legs to hold me in place; the gun was still in his hand, the tip covered in my wet, sticky pussy juices.

I gasped in pleasure as he slid his tongue inside me. It was long and extended well into my walls. Curling the tip of it, he tickled my g-spot until I cried out in ecstasy— He quickly clamped a hand over my mouth before I woke up his sister.

"*Ssh*," he whispered. "Shut yo' ass up…and let me lick on this pussy."

I moaned through his fingers as he began to suck on my clit, swirling around it with his tongue. I was breathing so heavy, it almost sounded like I was hyperventilating. Arching my back to meet his mouth, I savored the feel of his tongue as he plunged it deep inside me, lapping at my juices.

"*Oooh*, Sharif," I moaned.

I damn near lost it when he pressed his tongue in and out of me in sharp, stabbing motions. My hips bucked hard and desperately to keep up. By now, my juices were running out of his mouth and down his chin. He had me overflowing, and I felt my pussy clamp around his tongue as an orgasm shook through me.

Shadow was the only nigga capable of tongue-fucking me into a climax. He was also the only nigga to ever make me squirt, and I didn't hold back as I came all over his face and chin.

Shadow licked up every drop of cum, kissing my clit delicately in between. He felt me tense up a little, due to the sensitivity of my lady parts. It was always that way after a powerful orgasm.

Looking up from between my legs, he waited for me to come back down and get a hold of my senses. Our eyes met and his face broke into a huge smile. He knew the effect he had on me, and he knew that regardless of whatever bitch he was with, I would always have a place in his life.

"This my pussy..." he said, smacking it with his hand.

He made me squirt some more, and my body quaked with pleasure.

"Let me hear you say it," he whispered.

"This pussy is yours, Sharif. It'll always be yours."

Wrapping a hand around my throat, he pressed his thick, meaty dick against the opening of my pussy. It was still shimmering with wetness from cumming all over the place, but I wouldn't feel satisfied until he fucked me good and deep.

Moving the tip of his dick up and down my slit, he teased me unmercifully while making me wetter at the same time. Tilting his head back, he grunted completely consumed by ecstasy. Grasping my hips tightly, he slammed his full length into me in one sudden motion. His balls slapped my asshole as I cried out in pain and pleasure.

Pulling back, he did it again, fucking me slowly with long, hard strokes. I tried to meet his thrusts, but he just choked me harder and held me down. Shadow was an animal in the bedroom, and the nigga loved rough sex.

"You gon' let me cum in you?" he asked, filling me with slow torturous strokes. It'd been so long since the last time I had sex that he had to stretch me to fit his girth.

"I want you to," I moaned, not giving a fuck about the consequences.

He laughed and slammed into me, getting faster and faster until he was pounding me mercilessly.

"Shit, Shadow! FUCK!" I cried out. He had the headboard shaking, and my body on the verge of a second climax. As I climbed the peak, he reached up and started rubbing on my clit. That put me over the edge and once again, I came violently, digging my nails deep into his back.

"You mine," he grunted between thrusts. Without slowing down, he grabbed my bouncing tits and squeezed. "You hear me, bitch? You mine."

"Yes, baby," I moaned, as he kissed the side of my neck. He pinched and played with my nipples, still pounding me relentlessly.

He called out my name as he shot his load deep inside me. I came again, my tight pussy, milking his hard dick as he convulsed in pleasure. Panting harshly, he climbed off and slumped beside me in exhaustion.

"You should really let me clean those cuts," I offered.

"Sade can't know about this," he said.

"What? About us?" I asked, confused.

"I don't give a fuck about that. I'm talking about the shooting. I don't want her ass more worried than she already is. I get sick of hearing her bitch and complain. Sometimes I think she forgets she's my little sister. Not the other way around."

"She just doesn't want to see you hurt. But okay...I won't say anything." I said, raising my hands in surrender.

Shadow climbed off the bed and headed for the bathroom.

"Aye, Sharif," I called out.

"What?"

"Nigga, you owe me some money for some new sheets," I said, pointing to the stained covers.

Sharif turned around and grabbed his big, wet dick. "I got'cha money right here."

I laughed and threw a pillow at his head. On the real, this nigga had me loving his dirty muthafuckin' drawers.

17

Q

Heavy is the head that wears the crown.

—*Q*

Two days had passed since the shooting at one of our traps, and I was still on muthafuckin' red alert. I didn't leave the crib without it on me, and I made sure to watch my back wherever I went. I also had killas making rounds every hour, on the hour. My son and kid sister were usually home alone, and I couldn't risk something happening to them while a nigga was out in these streets.

Typically, I kept one shooter on standby at all times, but considering the circumstances, I had to put a couple more hittaz on my payroll. When you lived a fast life, you always had to be prepared for the unexpected. I had to keep an eagle out on these niggas if I ain't wanna get caught slipping. Speaking of caught slipping, I was still waiting on LaMar to get back the money he'd fucked around and lost. I was still pissed off at that nigga. We couldn't afford fuck ups. Not with the number of enemies that wanted to see us crash and burn.

If you don't have enemies, you're doing something wrong, Arlo would often say.

Suddenly, I spotted Arlo stumbling his old ass across the street. He lived a couple blocks away from my crib. I was on my porch, smoking a J, with a 12-gauge perched on my lap when I saw him. If a nigga decided to pull up on me again, this time I would be prepared.

"Aye, Arlo!" I called out, grabbing his attention. My Pitbulls started barking, and I yelled at their asses to quiet the fuck down. "Aye, Arlo! *Ven aca!*"

He always had the drop on some shit, and was my biggest source for intel. He was also the neighborhood drunk, and because of that, no one really considered him a threat. He was easily able to slip in and eavesdrop on shit undetected. I paid him to be my eyes and ears, and he dutifully kept me up on game.

Back in the day, he was a pusher and a pimp, but he fucked around and lost his leg to a rare disease.

Afterwards, it was like his life went downhill, and he started fucking around with that Lucy. The drugs caused him to lose touch of reality, and when they became too expensive for him to afford, he eventually turned to booze.

As a kid, I used to look up to the homie. I even cleared his debt with loan sharks to keep them from killing his ass. I looked out for mines, and I was one of the few who still had respect for dude, in spite of him losing his street cred.

I didn't give a fuck about all that shit though, Arlo was the first nigga to ever push a Bentley through my hood, and legend had it, he was once the richest muthafucka in Compton. He was a street legend then.

At six feet even, Arlo was brown-skinned, had gray eyes, and a balding hairline that he refused to let go of. His big ass nose was spread from east coast to west coast, and I often told the nigga he looked like Smokey Robinson. That shit always gassed him.

"Wuz brackin' wit' a YG though?" he asked, dapping me up. In his other hand was a Colt 45 can and a cigarette. He reeked of sweat, and his clothes were tattered, but by now I was used to his stench and appearance. With liquor stores piled on top of liquor stores, this was everyday life for a lot of folks in Compton. Sadly, my childhood hero had fallen victim to the same plight.

"Shit, my nigga, boolin'. I wanna holla at'chu 'bout somethin' though. Take a seat, real quick, blood." I pointed to the chair beside me.

"Wassup wit' it?"

"Shit, holding down the block." I adjusted the shotgun on my lap. "My nigga, tell me why some muthafuckas came to the trap to line me up."

"The Courts, over there in Watts?"

"Nah, my main spot." I had a few traps, but the only one worth robbing was in Compton. "Then on top of that, I find out my people's spot was hit just last night. My nigga, I don't know who they are. I don't know who sent' em. All I know is them niggas gotta go. Big homie, them niggas gotta feel something awful!" I stressed. "I need you to keep an ear out to who might have been behind that shit. The streets will be buzzing soon, and all it takes is one slip of the lip."

"They always do," he said. "I'll make sure to keep my ear to the streets."

Suddenly, a group of Mexicans came riding by the crib on horses. Those cost efficient muthafuckas would do anything to keep from spending money, including using horses for transportation.

"Them muthafuckas taking over, my nigga," he said, shaking his head. Arlo hated to see the very hood he once ran being reshaped before his very eyes, but there was little he could do but bitch, drink, and complain about it.

"How could you blame 'em. Them niggas band and break bread together. If we learned to stop hating on each other all the muthafuckin' time, niggas could take over some shit, too."

Arlo looked over and gave me a crooked grin. "You know sometimes I think you have a lot more potential than you let on. You bangin' now, but one day, you gon' drop yo flag and say fuck it."

"The day that happens, I'll be dropping to the ground with it," I said, throwing up my set. Live by the gun, die by the gun. That was my lifelong mentality.

Arlo laughed. "You say that now...but you're still young. You'll wake up one day and realize you don't wanna end up dead, or in jail...or like me. You breaking bread now, but don't get so caught up in the fast life, you forget your future. Don't get so caught up that you forget your son's future." He paused and sighed deeply. "I never told you this, but I have three sons of my own. Sons I never got the chance to teach baseball or football too. 'Cuz I was too busy in the streets, teaching hoes how to break a trick. I let the lifestyle take hold of me, and in turn it took my leg. There's not a day that goes by I don't regret the choices I made. There's not a day that goes by I don't regret being a part of my sons' lives, and really being there for 'em. Shit might be different than it is now. But it's too late for me," he said. "But it's not too late for you, young blood. The street game ain't designed for you to win. And it sure as shit don't come with a lifetime warranty."

"I hear you, my G."

Passing Arlo my blunt, I allowed his preaching ass to take a few puffs. "Oh, let me tell you 'bout this brazy ass shit that happened in Oakland, man." I laughed as the events came to mind. "My nigga, so why I'm at Shark Bar with the homie, and some bitch run smack into me, spilling my drink all over my jersey and shit. Brand new jersey at that, bruh. And instead of apologizing, the chick starts popping off like it's my fault. On blood, homie, I could've smacked the fuck out that hoe."

"Now I put my foot down to a bitch but I don't put my foot on a bitch. Ya dig what I'm sayin'?"

"Nah, I got'chu, pimpin'. It's just shorty had me so fucking heated. Then some shit went down, I tried to give the bitch a ride, and she flips the fuck out again. I swear, OG, the bitch touched several nerves of mine."

"But you want her," he continued with a raised brow. Arlo saw it all in my eyes and demeanor. He heard the telltale interest in my voice despite all the bullshit I was spilling.

I laughed in agreement. "Want her bad than a muthafucka. But I don't really know how to approach the shit. I mean, we ain't necessarily get off to a good start, ya feel me."

I wasn't really the romantic type. I tried to have a candlelit dinner at the crib once with my baby momma, and the entire place damn near caught on fire. That was the first and last time I ever tried to do some romantic shit.

Nowadays, some dick and some dollars was all these bitches got from me. But Sade wasn't the average bitch, and I wasn't trying to be on some average shit with her. I wanted her ass. Plain and simple. She made me realize that she was what I was missing in my life. And I knew that she wasn't that type of girl that you fed the dick to and left a 20 on the dresser. She was a legit good girl, and she deserved better.

"Let me tell you something my pops told me, young blood. When you see a woman, and *really* see something in her without really knowing her, then you know it's real. Regardless of starting off fucked up, if it's meant to be, it'll be," Arlo said.

I was just about to mention the phone when Kai opened the screen door, carrying my son Peace. I named him that because he brought some serenity into my world after he was born.

Peace took after Camari as far as complexion. He was dark brown with my eyes, and most of my features. When Peace spotted me on the porch, he gave a toothless grin and reached his arms out for me. He was 2, going on 3, and spoiled rotten, but that was all Kai's fault.

"Here, Q, take this lil' nigga," she said, shoving him into my arms. "His ass won't stop fussing and a bitch needs a fucking break."

Grabbing the shotgun, I laid it against my chair and took him from her. "Wassup, lil' man. What'chu fussin' 'bout now?" I asked him.

He tried to say that he wanted some candy but could barely pronounce the shit.

"See, that's why his damn teeth won't grow in now! He always wanna eat some damn candy and shit!" Kai complained.

Although Kai was my younger sister, she was 15 and a lesbian, who dressed and acted like one of the niggas. She wore her hair dreaded up, so people often mistook her for a little boy. She looked nothing like me. Kai was fair-skinned with good hair, a trait she'd inherited from her Dominican father. He was a married realtor who used to turn tricks with my mama in the 90s. Our mama worked the Blade before these new hoes were even thought of. She was that bitch too before they gunned her down in a sting. The cop that murdered her was never convicted, and I strongly believed it was because his ass was white.

A few riots preceded the events, but eventually things died down. Everyone moved on from it, and I was left to deal with the aftermath. I was only 11 at the time of her murder, and because we didn't know our fathers, I stepped up as the patriarchal figure. Kai's father couldn't be involved because he was a married man with his own family and his stupid ass didn't make his wife sign a prenup. He was afraid of her finding out about Kai, divorcing his ass, and taking all his money. I had no choice but to start selling drugs and banging as a means to take care of my family. The streets raised me, and I raised my sister.

I knew that was what our mother would've wanted. She wouldn't have wanted us split up in the system.

The gangs taught me how to get money. In the beginning, I used to think selling drugs was just a rich man's business, but I quickly learned that a nigga from the hood could take over. At only 21, I was moving hundreds of kilos of cocaine from state to state, and selling drugs to A-list actors. I had enough saved up to cover both Kai and Peace's college tuition. We were well off, and I knew mama would be proud.

She'd worked too hard to keep us together. She might've been a hoe, but she was the best that ever did it, and she went above and beyond to keep clothes on our backs and food in our stomachs. She taught me how to be a man. Something most people said women couldn't single-handedly accomplish. Now it was my job to protect my son and sister from the toxicity of a savage world.

Maybe that's why I fought so hard to get Camari off the streets. I didn't want what happened to my mom to happen to her, but it was obvious that taming Camari was a task beyond my capabilities. And honestly, I no longer had the energy to.

Besides, I had my eye on something new and a lot more promising...

***

After chopping it with my old head, I left Peace with my sister, and called an emergency meeting at our headquarters in Compton. It was actually an old drainage ditch that people now used as a skate park, but it was the perfect place for a congregation because it was tucked off in the cut. The walls were tagged in graffiti and gang signs, letting everyone know this was Blood territory.

"Now I know this was last minute, and I appreciate everyone for coming out," I began. "But I couldn't sleep on this shit...so a nigga had to call this meeting."

The crowd shuffled about nervously, as everyone struggled to figure out the reason for them being here. There were women, men, and even a few kids among the attendees, but everyone present shared the same vision as me. We all wanted to make money and we all wanted to take care of our families. But to continue doing that we had to first eliminate any competition.

LaMar was by my side, clutching a Mac 11 in front of him. I almost wanted to snatch that shit and empty the clip in his bitch ass. He still had yet to come up with the money that he'd lost. He claimed he was still working on it, and I prayed, for his sake, the issue was resolved. If he didn't get my money back soon, then I might have to handle his ass too. His mistakes were becoming cancerous, and like the disease, you had to cut out the cancer to get rid of it altogether.

The nigga was like my brother and all, but if I had to let him go to keep shit movin, then I would. At the end of the day, it was only business. As a leader, I had a huge responsibility of making sure everyone ate. I couldn't do that if he was constantly screwing up.

Standing on the highest part of the ramp, I took in the sight of all the red shirts and red bandanas before me. They all looked to me as their leader, seeing as how I brought prosperity to the hood. Because of me, no one was starving or missing any meals. Everyone had a role, everyone played their position, and everyone moved like brothers and sisters. I was the one that gave orders to them all, but that didn't make shit any less easy on me.

Heavy is the head that wears the crown. That was the realest shit Arlo had ever told me.

"Now as you all may've heard, we had a situation a couple days ago. A situation that led to one of our traps being robbed." I didn't even want to mention the $425,000 LaMar had fucked around and lost.

Chatter immediately erupted, with people saying they knew the culprits and others threatening to punish them. But until we found out who was behind them hits, they were all just empty ass threats.

"EVERYBODY SHUT THE FUCK UP AND LISTEN!" I ordered.

Because of the respect they had for me, the chatter instantly died down.

"Now I don't know who was behind this shit. But I know them niggas gon' get brought to justice. In the meantime, I need every one of ya'll to stay on ya toes! Move cautiously. We can't afford to take any more Ls. Now I already got ears to the streets, but I need everyone to keep their eyes open."

"We wouldn't have to if this pussy ass nigga wasn't playing for both teams!" a random guy in the crowd shouted out. Before I could question him, he kicked the guy in front of him in the ass, causing him to stumble forward and be seen. "This fuck nigga a rat!" he yelled. "I wouldn't be surprised if his snitch ass told them niggas where the spot was at. Think about it. We been running these blocks for years with no real issues. As soon as we bring this nigga in, then all of a sudden, it's a problem!"

"He right, Q," another chimed in. "Homie *been* fishy. I heard he was a Crip before he did that lil' bid in Juvie. Then he came home, and started banging blood. Who's to say he ain't playing both sides?"

"C'mon, Q. You know me! You know that's not facts!" the young boy argued. He was 17, and a new face to the family, but trustworthy nonetheless.

"So, what part of it is true?" I asked him. The entire crowd was silent as they waited on his response.

The kid hesitated, looked around for someone to help, then dropped his gaze to the floor when he realized no one would. "I mean…I *was* one…before I got locked up. That part of it is true," he admitted. "But that was a different life then, man. It was a different time. A different me."

Disappointed by the news, I climbed off the ramp and slowly approached him. The crowd gradually parted as a path was created for me. No one said a word; they only watched and waited in anticipation.

"Please, Q," he begged. "You gotta understand, man. It was a different time then. People change…"

Tired of the excuses, I stripped him of his flag. "Yeah, you right. And we can't afford that, either."

The moment, I turned my back on him, everyone in the crowd started attacking him. Screams pierced the air as he was punched, kicked, and stomped on. Even the kids jumped in and started whupping his muthafuckin' asss. With sixty or so people fighting to get a piece of him, he was sure to be killed on the very turf that he swore by. But that was the consequence of being a deceitful traitor.

Everyone knew the punishment for treachery was an automatic death penalty. I refused to trust anyone affiliated with my enemies.

Tat! Tat! Tat! Tat! Tat! Tat! Tat! Tat!

Suddenly, LaMar released a few rounds in the air, making everyone stop what they were doing. He must've felt sympathy for the kid, because he climbed off the ramp, and put two shots in his chest, sparing him a painful death.

I always said that nigga had a bigger heart than mine.

***

Later that night, I found myself in my makeshift office, thinking about Sade. I wanted to holla at her real quick to take my mind off all of the bullshit. Even though he was a traitor, I felt bad for killing that kid. It really took a lot out of me and right now, I just wanted to hear her voice.

I had already called myself with her phone the night I found it in my car, so I had her number for quite a while. Now it was time to put that muthafucka to use. Sitting down at the desk, I pushed the inventory papers out of the way to access my computer keyboard. I then typed her number into Yellow Pages' search engine. A photography company she owned immediately popped up. It was a small business with only a few reviews, but all of them were stellar.

Elegant Rose Artistry was the name of her company, and it had only been up and running for almost 2 years now. She'd graduated from the *New York Film Academy* in LA, and had aspirations of owning a studio, but for now, she did freelance work.

A smart girl with a good head on her shoulders. It was nice to know she was striving for something. Nowadays, that seemed like a rare find. Most bitches I knew sold pussy for a living.

On a whim, I decided to call her to see if her line was back on. Much to my surprise, she answered on the third ring. "Hello?" Her beautiful voice filled the receiver, and in that instant, I forgot my inhibitions.

"I see you replaced the phone."

"I see you were determined to hang onto it," she retorted. "Seriously, it took you three whole days to contact me?"

I paused and scratched my chin. "What can I say? A nigga was tied up."

"And so am I... Now what do you want?"

"You," I simply said, as I smiled into the phone.

"*Excuse me*?!" she asked, offended.

I quickly recovered. "You ain't let me finish. I want you to do a shoot for my son's birthday party. It's two weeks from today. It pays well, and I can even wire you a deposit now to secure the date."

"How'd you know I was a—never mind, it doesn't even matter. I can't, 'cuz I'm already booked up—"

"Well, free up some space then. This shit is important to me."

"And so are my other clients who've also secured their dates."

"I'll pay double whatever they're paying on top of mine."

"What's with you? You always think it's about the money. It's not always about the money, Q—"

"Sit on it. Can you do that for me? I'll hit you in a couple days to see if you made a decision."

Sade sighed into the receiver, as if I were asking her to donate a kidney. "I'll think about it," she finally agreed.

It wasn't a flat out yes, but shit, it was good enough for me.

18

LaMar

"I thought we were past that shit."

—*LaMar*

"How can I help you, sir?" the clerk asked with a friendly smile. She was a cute, young Mexican chick that always rushed to assist me whenever I came through. The bitch was on my dick like a condom, but I would never give her ass any play. I liked my women like I liked my chicken. Dark.

"Uh, lemme get a bottle of D'Ussé."

"The three seventy-five, or the seven-fifty?"

"Lemme get that big boy," I said, handing her a Franklin.

Knowing me, I'd probably run through the whole bottle in one night. I had some shit on my mind, like how I was gone get back that cash Camari took. My young niggas were combing the streets for that nigga, but ever since Romello got his hands on the cash, the nigga was in ghost mode. No one saw or heard from him, even his hoes had disappeared off the track. LA was only so big. His ass could run, but he couldn't hide.

I knew shit was shaky between me and Q ever since I lost that bread. It wasn't so much about the money as it was me being unreliable. He was thorough when it came to doing shit, so one slip up to him was unacceptable.

"Here's your change. Would you like the receipt?"

"Nah, you keep that," I said, turning the $47 away.

"Thank you. I appreciate it. Have a good night."

"You too, mamí."

I was on my way out the door when I noticed a familiar face walking in. She was eyeing me too like she remembered me, but couldn't recall from where. "I see you peaking and not speaking."

Her chocolate, fine ass stopped and pulled her sunglasses off. "Carjacker, is that you?" She asked.

"Real funny. I thought we were past that shit."

"Nigga, you were past that. I never said that I was."

"Yeah, well, you sure spent that muthafuckin' money, now didn't you?"

"I sure did," she smiled. "You like?" Jayda spun around in her two-piece denim set. She had a white fuzzy Kango hat on her head, and on her pretty feet was a pair of strap up heels. She was thicker than a snicker, and the way her ass sat up in them jeans made my dick hard. There was nothing more that I wanted than to bend her black ass over. I had a thing for imported chocolate.

"Yeah, I like it. But I'm more interested in what's underneath."

"Tuh...You'll never find out." She scoffed at me

I licked my lips and stepped closer. "Oh yeah. How much you wanna bet?"

"Nigga, how much *you* wanna bet?" she challenged.

"I bet my trap I'll fuck you in this store right now, yo thick ass keep playin' with me. You know I'm on yo head. A nigga got a muthafuckin' sweet tooth."

"Alright, you gone fuck around and catch a cavity." She smiled that beautiful smile of hers. I don't think I'd ever seen such perfect teeth.

"I'll take that risk. Anyway, what'chu finna get into?"

"I was about to grab a bottle of D'Ussé and head back to the crib."

I held up my bag. "You may as well come fuck with me. We could bust this bitch down together, and you could let me know a lil' about you."

"Oh, now you wanna know about me? Last I checked I was a bum ass bitch."

"Man, that be that liquor talking. My bad for that bullshit I said. Can you find it in your heart to forgive me? A nigga really tryin' to fuck wit'chu, on some real shit."

"I don't know. Let me think about it." She put her finger on her chin. "Uh, no."

She tried to walk off, but I grabbed her wrist and stopped her.

"Nigga, we ain't got shit else to discuss."

"We got plenty to discuss."

"Like what?"

"Like what your favorite position is."

"Nigga, bye. I told your ass you ain't getting none of this."

***

"*Oooh*, damn, get that shit!" Jayda moaned.

Holding her leg in the air by her ankle, I fucked the dog shit out her thick ass. Pussy was so good, I wasn't even gon' hold her to the bet.

"I'mma make you cum in every position," I groaned in her ear. "And hopefully that'll be enough to make you forgive me." Massaging her clit, I fucked her senseless. "Damn this pussy wet, ma."

"That's all you," Jayda moaned out.

The faster I moved in and out of her, the more she threw her ass back to meet my strokes. "Damn, this shit gushing," I whispered, as her pussy cream foamed up my dick.

Turning her over on her side, I spooned my way inside of her. She was so damn wet, I said to hell with the muthafuckin' condom. I needed to feel this bitch. As her body tensed up, I picked her leg up and lifted it in the air as I pushed deep inside of her.

"Oooh, shit, LaMar," she moaned. With her leg in the crook of my arm, I moved to her clit and started rubbing it while I was fucking her.

Jayda started bucking her hips to meet my match as I started going faster and faster in and out of her. "I love you, baby," she blurted out in the midst of all the pleasure. This good dick had her ass saying all type of crazy shit.

"I love you too, baby," I said for the hell of it.

"Oh, I'm cumming baby!" she cried out.

"Give me that pussy, girl," I moaned as she began to buck harder. "Cum on this dick, baby."

"Shit!" she cried as her body trembled with intense pleasure.

I was right behind her. As I pumped harder, I felt my nut building up as I grabbed hold of Jayda's waist and thrust my hips harder. "*Ahhh*, fuck!" I groaned, emptying my seeds deep inside of her. I collapsed behind her as we tried to catch our breath, and before I knew it, we both had dozed off.

19

Jayda

"Nigga, ain't nobody touching this pussy but you."

-Jayda

"So, you just smash and dip on a nigga, huh?" LaMar asked after waking up and finding me getting dressed. He was still lying on his bed in all his naked glory.

"I'm not dipping, nigga," I sassed him as I struggled to pull my jeans over my voluptuous ass. "I hadn't even planned to be here, I do have shit to do today." I told him.

"Yeah, a'ight." He smirked as he lit a blunt that had been sitting on the night stand. "Well, when you're done doing '*your shit*' how bout you slide back through and we crack open that bottle, finally," he said gesturing towards the unopened bottle of D'Ussé.

As soon as we walked through the door of his place, shit got real and we completely neglected the alcohol.

"Maybe." I grinned at him over my shoulder as I finished getting dressed. I gathered my things and headed back to my car.

Once I got home, I noticed that I had several missed calls from Shadow. Frowning at my phone, I prepared to call him back. He never blew me up like this, unless he was beefing with that bitch Tia. I couldn't stand her stankin' ass. Because Shadow and I could never be public with our relationship, that stankin' ass bitch took every chance to rub theirs in my face, especially because I'm sure she suspected something was going on with me and her 'technical' man. She was older than me and Shadow at 26, she had 3 kids by three different guys and swore she was some high class stay at home mom. Bitch was a fucking welfare queen, but even I had to admit she was bad as hell. To have three kids, she had not one stretch mark in sight and she had a figure to die for. I could definitely see why Shadow was attracted to her, but that didn't stop me from hating the bitch's guts though.

"Bitch, why you ain't been answering my calls?" Shadow barked into the phone as soon as he answered it.

"Well hello to you too, nigga!" I shot back sarcastically. Everyone was so afraid of Shadow and nobody challenged him the way that I did.

"Bitch, I know you ain't out here giving my pussy away," he said with a menacing tone.

I got quiet as I thought about what I'd just been doing with LaMar. "No, of course not," I said before I paused too long.

"Yeah, let me find out, that's yo muthafuckin' ass," he threatened.

Shadow had been my first everything. I'd even held him down while he did his bid. I didn't know why I fucked LaMar in the heat of the moment like that. It just happened. I was praying Shadow never found out. He already wasn't fond of my infatuation with Romello, and there was no chance of me getting with him. He'd probably try to kill me if he found out I'd actually fucked another nigga.

Scratch that, he would kill me.

"Nigga, ain't nobody touching this pussy but you," I said trying to lay it on thick. "But I'm sure the same can't be said about you," I told him pointedly.

"Aye, don't worry about what I'm touching. As long as I'm touching you, you should be happy," he said.

"Yes daddy," I purred into the phone. "Am I gone see you tonight?" I asked him with desperation in my voice.

"I got some shit to handle tonight, but if I finish in time, I might try to slide through on you," he told me.

"Okay...I'ma hold you to it, nigga."

"You do that, keep it tight for me," he said before hanging up the phone.

Boy, if he only knew.

20

Shadow

"Strike the shepherd and the sheep will scatter."

—Dreeco

After hanging up the phone with Jayda, I turned my attention back to the task of counting the money from my most recent lick. I almost shot the homie Dreeco by accident when he walked in the trap wearing a red jersey and Indians hat. Placing the Beretta back down on the kitchen table, I resumed putting bundles of cash into the money counting machine. We were eating off the lick we'd hit a couple nights ago. Now that I made my come up, I was about to get back in the streets heavy with it.

Instead of hitting Q's spot, we ended up robbing one of his affiliate gangs, known as Tree Top Piru. They were located in the north region of Compton, and sold work for Q on three of the major corners: Rosecrans Avenue, Aranbe Avenue, and Acacia Avenue.

Even with everything we'd grabbed, we still didn't get nearly as much as we would have hitting Q's spot. That muthafucka had gotten lucky, but soon his luck would run out. "Aye, wuz good, Dreeco. You got the dime on that nigga, or what?" I asked, dapping him up.

"Hell yeah...I went to that nigga's lame ass faggot fest. Man, you should've seen that nigga, standing at the top of a ramp, gassed up on his own bitch ass ego. On the dead homie, it took everything in me not to kill that nigga."

The plan was for Dreeco to infiltrate their gang, and see what the fuck they were planning at this meeting he'd called. Q had no idea that one of his own enemies was among the attendees. "So, what the fuck was that slob ass nigga hollerin' about?"

"Man, that nigga wasn't 'bout nothing. Nigga weak than a bitch. He ain't got a clue who was behind them hits. But aye, I say we move on that nigga while he struggling to figure shit out," he laughed. "I fucked him all up when I kicked this nigga in front of me. Man, you should've seen that shit. I kicked the lil' homie right in his ass," he bragged. "I started pointing the finger at him, saying that we couldn't trust him because he was a snitch, and then everyone else starting jumping on board. Man, I made that nigga Q kill his own fucking people. I ain't 'een know homie. I just made up some bullshit, and that nigga ran with it. Homie got the heart, but not the smarts. If he'll fall that easy for the okie dokie, think how simple it'll be to get rid of his ass."

I nodded my head in agreement. "And that's *real* shit."

"Like my pops use to say, strike the shepherd and the sheep will scatter."

21

Sade

"Do I really wanna get mixed up with a nigga like him?"

—*Sade*

The following afternoon, Jayda surprised me with a trip to the most upscale salon in Hollywood Hills. She paid for us to get our hair and nails done, and in between we chatted about life's latest happenings.

"So, who the fuck was you screwing the other night?" I asked, as we soaked our feet in a pedicure bowl. We each wore roller sets in our head, and white wrapping strips to mold down the gel.

"On God! You could hear that?" Jayda gasped with her hand over her mouth, clearly embarrassed.

"Bitch, how could I not? I think the whole neighborhood heard that shit!"

Her cheeks flushed in humiliation and she tapped her chin as she thought up a lie. "Bitch, you ain't gon' believe this shit...But that was all me. I ain't even have no nigga over the other night. Just a date with three of my fingers and some lube—"

"*Eww*, hoe, TMI!"

"You so fucking stupid, Jay," Toucan laughed. He was our stylist, and long-time friend. We'd met while working on the sets of a few mutual clients. He was always gossiping, and had the scoop on everything and everyone in the industry. But he was my homeboy and I loved his messy ass. "I hope you at least washed them thangs before coming here," he said.

Jayda shoved her hand in his face. "Wanna smell 'em?"

"Ugh, girl, no! Them thangs smell like dick and disappointment, honey!"

Me and Jayda both laughed at that one.

"Girl, so tell me why Q hit my line the other day."

"*Whaaaattt*??? He called you?" Jayda asked, wide-eyed and surprised. I finally told her that I'd lost my phone after realizing I left it in his car. "Damn, Q ain't backing down, is he."

"*Unh-unh*. Who is this Q?" Toucan asked, waving around his comb. "And why haven't you mentioned him to me?" He lived for being in other people's business, but that was the norm when you worked in a salon.

"This guy I met in Oakland during All Star Weekend. It's nothing serious. He gave me a ride home and I accidentally left my phone in his car."

"Bitch, that can't be *all* there is to him. Stop being stingy and give us the 411!" Toucan urged. "Is he cute? Is he funny? Does he have a big dick?"

"Damn! I don't know. Like I said, it's nothing serious. I just met the man."

Toucan frowned at me. "You don't even know if he cute, bitch? Damn, you're no fun."

I smiled and shrugged. "I mean, yeah. He's cute...in a rough, thuggish sort of way."

"*Mmm*. Toucan love the thugs." He said popping his hip out, and snapping his fingers.

"Boy, you love anything with swinging meat between its legs."

Toucan clutched his heart and batted his eyelashes at Jayda. "Bitch, you know me well."

"*Anyway*," I laughed. "He called me last night to see if I could do a photoshoot for his son in two weeks."

"*And*? You got the availability, right?" Jayda asked.

"Of course, I got the availability. Bitch, I haven't been booked in months. The money I spent in Oakland was just a temporary loan from my father. Bitch, I'm MC Hammer broke! I need this gig but—"

"But what?" Jayda pressed.

"I don't know, girl. It's...*him*. Like is it really a good idea to agree to doing it? We saw the type of shit he be into when he started that riot in the club. Do I really wanna get mixed up with a nigga like him? Dealing with Shadow is enough—and that's family," I pointed out.

"Girl, it's just a photoshoot!" she laughed. "You act like he's asking to initiate you into a gang. Do the shoot, get the money, and be done with it. It's as simple as that..." she paused. "Although, I'm sure you don't really want to be done with it."

Before I could respond, a fine, buff ass mailman walked in, carrying envelopes and packages for the shop owner. "Hey, is Jessica in?" he asked.

"No, she's out right now, honey," Toucan said. "But you can leave that with me, and I'll make sure she gets 'em." His eyes lit up with lust, and there was a hint of flirtation in his tone. The poor mailman looked terrified, but he brought the packages over as Toucan had requested. "*Mmm.* Look at you, handsome. What your name is?"

"Toucan, stop. You're scaring him," Jayda giggled.

"Shit, he scaring me! I ain't never seen nobody this damn fine before!"

The mailman laughed, taking it all in good stride. "My name's Sam," he said, holding his hand out to shake.

Toucan shook his hand with grace. "Nice to meet you, Sam. They call me Toucan."

Sam looked confused. "And why do they call you that?"

"'Cuz two can play this game, honey. I can either be a lady...or I can be a *nigga*," he said, deepening his voice. "Whichever you prefer," he flirted wickedly.

Growing uncomfortable, Sam released his hand. "Can you make sure Jessica gets these?"

Toucan batted his long lashes. "Will do."

"Thanks, 'preciate it. Have a good day, ladies."

Everyone in the shop bidded his fine ass farewell, including Toucan who couldn't stop staring as the mailman walked away.

"And you called me, stupid," Jayda laughed. "Boy, you hella ignant!" She was beyond amused by the entire scenario, and couldn't stop cracking up.

"Girl, I just want the drumstick and nothing else," he said.

"Alright now, Rodney gon' kill your ass if he finds out you're cheating on him." Jayda reminded him.

"When your pussy's as good as mine, it's hard not to cheat," he said.

"I'll be sure to engrave that in your tombstone," I told him.

"*Anyway*," Jayda cut in. "If my opinion holds any weight, I really think you should do it."

"Do what?" I asked, incredulously.

"The photoshoot. Duh."

"Oh...yeah...that," I said, growing slightly nervous. I don't know why Q had that effect on me. "You really think I should?"

"It shouldn't even be a question, bitch. You need the money, and from what you just told me, you need to pay back your father. There's no law that prohibits cops from arresting their daughters."

I laughed. "Over a loan though."

"Shit, you know how yo daddy be."

Jayda was right. I needed the cash, and the credit for my portfolio. I also needed to see Q one last time to know if I still felt the same way about him. One thing was for certain; I felt giddy as fuck on the phone when I first heard his voice. That deep, smooth, even-toned voice got me every time. There was no wrong way for him to say anything.

Damn him for getting in my head, I cursed.

In spite of the façade I put on, I was really feeling Q...and it was nice to know he was feeling me, too.

***

After leaving the salon, Jayda and I had lunch and parted ways, and then it hit me. She was being awfully sneaky lately. Always dipping off and locking herself in her room, fucking somebody. She definitely wasn't jacking off like she tried to play earlier. Just as I walked into my apartment, I heard the phone start to ring. Rushing over to it, I checked the caller ID and saw that it was my father calling.

I took a deep breath to compose myself before answering. I loved my daddy with all my heart, but he could be so rigid sometimes. I swear, between him and Freddy I'm surprised I had an identity of my own.

"Hello," I finally answered just before the answering machine picked up.

"Hey, baby girl. When were you going to tell me that you were involved in a shoot-out? Or was I supposed to read about it in the obituaries?" he questioned me.

"Daddy, nobody was involved in a shoot-out! How do you even know about that?" I asked.

"One of my colleagues down in Oakland told me about how your roommate's name came up on the report. I don't know how many times I have to tell you, following that ignorant ass hood rat will always get you into trouble!" he fussed at me.

"Daddy, Jayda didn't have anything to do with the shoot-out. She was an innocent bystander that got hit by a stray bullet. She could have died and you're calling her a hood rat."

"Yeah, well no one would miss her," he mumbled.

"Daddy! That's my best friend you're talking about" I shouted trying to defend Jayda. "I know you didn't just call me to belittle my roommate. How can I help you, sir?" I asked him trying to cut to the fucking chase.

"Freddy called me..." he started.

"Oh, here we go with this bullshit." I slipped and said.

"Watch your mouth, young lady. You might be grown, but you will show your father some damn respect," he stated sternly.

"Look daddy, I'm sorry for cursing but I don't need Freddy running to you and tattling on me like some little baby. Childish sh—stuff like that definitely doesn't make me want to be with him." I rambled, catching myself before I cursed again. "Honey, I know you're young, but Freddy is a good fit for you. He's ambitious, he's well off, he can support you—"

"I can support myself," I said, cutting him off.

"Oh yeah, by taking your little pictures??" He scoffed in disgust.

It killed my daddy that I didn't want to be a lawyer, or enter some other corporate job. I was always creative, and artsy. Once I picked up a camera, I could never put it back down. I just knew that photography was my calling. And it damn near destroyed my daddy that I answered it. The only reason I was even able to go to film school was because I'd won an art scholarship after being encouraged by my high school counselor. My father had flat out refused to pay for it.

"Yes, with my little pictures, daddy." I mocked him.

"And when was the last time you had a paying job, huh?" he asked me.

"I have one coming up, a good paying one. To shoot some big wigs kid's birthday party." I said referring to Q's offer to shoot his son's party. I couldn't believe how effortlessly I let that lie roll off my tongue.

"Oh, is that so?" he asked me skeptically.

"Yes, daddy. I love you, but you and Freddy cannot just run my life and expect me to fall in line. Look, I just walked in the door. I have to go. I'll talk to you later, daddy," I said, before quickly hanging up the phone. I stood there for a few minutes, thoughts of my father and Freddy rolling around in my mind before I picked the phone back up and dialed a number.

"Hello," he picked up and his sultry voice flowed through the phone, and went right down my spine.

"Q, I'll gladly shoot your son's birthday party." I said before my confidence wore off and I backed out.

"Shit, you ain't said nothing but a word," he said.

22

Camari

"In the midst of it all were 2 hoes trying to break a trick."

—*Camari*

You ain't gotta say too much…

From the look in your eyes…I can tell you want to fuck…

And you ain't gotta call me ya boo…Just as bad as you wanna fuck…

I wanna fuck too…

504 Boyz "*I Can Tell*" poured through the built in custom speakers of the Beverly Hills mansion I was in. Me and my white bitch Chelsie were twerking on each other butt ass naked, putting on a freaky ass show for the baller we'd snagged on Rodeo Drive. We were on our way inside

the Gucci store when I purposely bumped into his rich ass to get his attention.

The second he laid eyes on us, he wanted us. I put a price and time on it, and we met at his crib right after he sent his wife of on a spa retreat. Now that he had the whole place to himself, we had that bitch lit. Pills, cocaine lines, and liquor bottles were scattered everywhere, and in the midst of it all were 2 hoes trying to break a trick.

His name was Paul, and he was middle-aged judging from his salt and pepper hair. Tall with a broad build, he had a big belly from eating good. He owned several of the medical cannabis dispensaries in Los Angeles, and ever since they passed the state law in '96, his business had been booming.

Paul's ass was filthy stinking rich. You could tell just by the way he lived. In all my life, I don't think I'd ever been in a bigger and more lavish home. He had a plunge pool and wet bar in the living room, and a hot tub and mini bar in the back. The walls were floor to ceiling windows that stretched around his entire home, and they offered magnificent views of the city and the mountains. His house was absolutely breathtaking. Paul had some money, and a real hoe like me knew how to get it.

Put me on the counter in the kitchen...

Now baby pour my body with some ice cream...

Lick me from head to toe...Bending me over...

69 will be the next thing...

I wanna taste your body all night long...

From sun up to sundown, I wanna make you moan...

Positioned over Chelsie, I popped my ass to the beat of the song. Paul was cheesing from ear to ear and nodding his head to the music. His white ass didn't listen to this shit on any other occasion, but he was drunk, high and horny. A dangerous combination when you were dealing with two sheisty hoes like us.

You ain't gotta say too much...

From the look in your eyes...I can tell you want to fuck...

And you ain't gotta call me ya boo...

Just as bad as you wanna fuck…

I wanna fuck too…

Spanking my ass, I gave him a seductive look. "How you like that, daddy?" I asked him. "That ass fat enough for you?"

He stroked his small dick through his boxers and wet his lips. "*Mmm.* It's too much for me to handle," he said. "Bend over. Let me see that pretty, pink pussy."

Grabbing Chelsie's shoulders for leverage, I tooted my ass in the air so he could get a glimpse at my va-jay-jay. It was unshaven but that only seemed to make his dick harder.

"Yeah…now I wanna see you kiss that pretty, black pussy," he told Chelsie.

Laughing drunkenly, she turned around and started sucking on my clit. She ate my pussy all the time so this was nothing new to her.

"Yeah, that's it…" he said, jerking faster. "Lick that pussy, baby. Stick your tongue in her hole. As far as it'll go."

Rubbing my clit harder, I started riding her face and pulling on her hair. I was just about to cum when suddenly, he said some crazy shit.

"Piss in her mouth."

An invisible record scratched and me and Chelsie looked up at him in confusion. Neither one of us expected to hear that odd request. *I swear white folks are some nasty muthafuckas*, I thought to myself.

"Lemme find out you into watersports," I laughed.

He continued to stroke his cock. "I'm into all types of kinky shit, baby."

"I see that."

Chelsie wiped her mouth and straightened up.

"Well, if we gone do all that, I'mma need some H2O first. Mind if I grab a glass of water?" I inquired.

"Help yourself, baby. You know where the kitchen is. Just don't be long," he said.

"I'll keep you busy in the meantime," Chelsie said, taking him in her mouth. She sucked his dick like a porn star as I took a detour on my way to the kitchen. I didn't need a glass of water. I needed every piece of jewelry he had up in this muthafucka.

Tiptoeing upstairs, I searched the home for his bedroom. From the second floor, I could hear him moaning and telling Chelsie to lick his nuts. If she could preoccupy him long enough, I'd be able to look for valuables and anything else worth cashing in on. Normally, I didn't rob tricks, but it was rare to come across ones that were as rich as Paul. I had to take advantage of this shit, because moments like these didn't come often.

Bingo!

I stopped in the doorway of his bedroom, and spotted a Rolex on the nightstand. Claiming it for myself, I searched his draws for the rest of his time pieces and jewelry. After pocketing a few rings, and lesser expensive watches, I made my way to his walk-in closet. There was a large safe inside located on the top shelf, and I figured something of even greater value had to be inside. Why else would he keep it locked away?

Before I could reach for it, I heard a gun cock behind me. When I turned around, I found Paul holding a pistol to Chelsie's head.

"You can never trust a bitch!" he spat.

Chelsie cried and trembled as he held her. I could tell that she never expected the night to end like this. Hell, I never even saw this shit coming. I was certain that he was too high and preoccupied to notice my departure. But I guess that's why they say you shouldn't assume. That fatal mistake could potentially cost me my life.

"All you black bitches are the same! The second I turned my back, you—"

WHAP!

Paul's sentence was cut short after Romello clocked him with his gun. His body fell forward before landing with a hard thud. I wasted no time grabbing the gun from him, but it was pointless considering he was out cold. I almost forgot that he was keeping an eye out front, unbeknownst to Paul.

Romello's niggas quickly came and ransacked the place. It was a free-for-all as everyone took designer clothes, shoes, antique pieces, vintage wine bottles, and his safe. Nothing was off limits. Romello kept the pills and the zip for himself. That in itself was valued at over than 20 grand. Me and Chelsie split the jewelry and the $2000 he'd given us prior.

"Fuck we gon' do with this piece of shit?" I asked, kicking Paul's torso.

Romello lit up a blunt. "Fuck you wanna do with him?"

I pointed Paul's pistol at his unconscious body. "I could think of a few things. Like dumping his ass in a lake somewhere." I kicked Paul again. "Piece of shit called me a black bitch! The fuck? On God, this nigga gotta go."

"Shit, do what'chu gotta do," Romello said, pointedly.

I squeezed and released two rounds into him.

POP!

POP!

After putting 2 slugs in his back, we cleared out his garage, taking every luxury vehicle he owned. We then fled the mansion before the police arrived. We could already hear them in the distance. Luckily, we'd be long gone by the time they showed up to the murder scene.

Burning rubber, Romello raced his homies in Paul's blue Lamborghini, and Chelsie and I whipped his black Mercedes S-class.

We were all high and geeked off the lick, driving past the speed limit in the suburbs of California. It was moments like these I lived for. They made me feel alive; not like the sorry, worthless, piece of shit mom that I was. My son's birthday was in a couple weeks, and this was the first time he'd crossed my mind in months. I was so busy living in the fast lane, that I lost track of what I *should* be living for.

"Bitch, I can't believe you rocked that muthafucka to sleep!" Chelsie said, interrupting my thoughts. She was in the passenger seat with her window down and her hair blowing in the wind. "I swear, seeing you pull that trigger made my muthafuckin' pussy wet!"

"I don't believe you," I laughed.

She slid a hand down the front of her pants, dipped two fingers inside, then smeared them across my face. "You believe me now, bitch?" she asked seductively as she pushed her fingers into my mouth, so I could suck them clean.

Her pussy juices began to dry against my skin. That freaky shit really turned me on. "You my muthafuckin' bitch. Bring your sexy ass here, and gimme a kiss," I said, taking my eyes off the road. She stuck her tongue in my mouth, and I almost crashed trying to suck on that bitch.

"Damn! Be careful! Don't run these hoes down!" she said, pointing to a block of old washed up hookers. A few years ago, that used to be us, but I forgot that shit in an instant.

Pulling alongside a broke-down bum ass bitch, I lowered my window and called out to her. "Aye, hoe! Say, hoe! You trying to get this paper, though?" I laughed. She wasn't much to look at, but from what I could see, she had a bit of potential—with the right amount grooming, of course.

Instead of being flattered by my interest, she stuck her middle finger up in anger. "Bitch, get the fuck on 'fore I beat the dog living shit out'cho ass!"

"You washed up street hoe! Fuck you!" Without thinking, I grabbed my can of mace and started pepper-spraying that slut.

"Broke ass hoe! Choose up!" Chelsie yelled out the window as we pulled away.

POP!

POP!

I let two rounds go at the sky with the gun I'd killed Paul with. We both couldn't stop laughing at her stupid ass crying on the corner. High as fuck, and on some other shit, I wasn't aware of my surroundings. When Chelsie finally screamed for me to slow down, it was already too late.

BOOOOOOM!

Our car slammed into the back of a police cruiser, causing our bodies to jerk forward. My head split open after cracking my shit on the steering wheel. Blood seeped into my eyes, but I could still see the sirens flashing.

Touching the gaping wound in the center of my head, I realized that I needed stitches. Suddenly, the cop climbed out of his car, and I knew right then, that a bitch had bigger problems.

23

Sade

"Jealousy consumed me and I hated her ass without even knowing her name."

—*Sade*

Keeping my eyes on the road, I tried to ignore the suspicious stares I got as I drove by the store that burned down in the riots. A group of Bloods were shooting dice in front of it, but their game immediately paused when they saw my blue van. Ironically, it was the same store my mom was murdered in, and it unsettled me to be in this area again.

I was in west Compton, on my way to Q's crib for his son's birthday party. I had agreed to shoot for the event, but unfortunately, I was running behind thanks to Shadow forgetting to put gas in the van. *What a terrible way to start a business relationship*, I thought. It wasn't like me to be unprofessional.

"I hope I wrote down the right address." I became uneasy when those same group of Bloods waved their guns at me. They probably would've shot at my ass, too, if I hadn't hit the corner.

I was sure that most of the stares were attributed to the color of my van. But it was all my little money could afford at the time, so for now, it would have to do. When I finally reached the end of the street, I spotted a telephone pole with red balloons wrapped around it. I could hear the music playing and I sighed in relief, thankful that I'd finally made it to his place—alive.

Lil Bow Wow's *"Bounce With Me"* was playing on full blast and kids were running around everywhere. There were bubbles, balloons, animals, trampolines, blow up slides, clowns and magicians for entertainment. This was by far the most lit kids' party I'd ever been to, and I knew that Q had paid a pretty penny to have it.

Speaking of Q, I aimlessly wandered through the crowd in search of him. *Damn. Maybe I should pop some gum before I get all up in his grill.* Digging in my purse, I pulled out a fresh pack of Spearmint. Before I could open it, I felt a small hand tug on my dress. When I looked down,

I realized it was the guest of honor himself. I could tell right away because of all the Franklins pinned to his shirt.

"You must be the birthday boy," I said, kneeling in front of him. "My name is Sade. What's yours?"

Instead of answering, the little boy gave a toothless grin and pointed to my gum.

"Come here, man. You know you don't need that shit," Q said, swooping the child up in his arms. He tore off the sides to an Icee foam cup and handed it to his son. I didn't even see him walk up, so I was still perched on the floor when he arrived. Ironing out the wrinkles in my sundress, I stood to my feet and greeted him. "Hi."

"You're late."

"I know. My stupid brother—"

"You're here, so it don't matter. It means a lot that you even came." Q leaned in and gave me a hug, and I immediately got butterflies in my tummy.

"No problem."

When we pulled apart, I noticed his son had picked the gum off of me.

"You don't want that little man. Besides, I've got something much cooler for you." I handed him a Hot Wheels set and his eye lit up with excitement.

"That's love right there. I appreciate it, and so does he. Say thank you, man," Q urged his son. "Show the lady your manners."

"*Thank youuu!*" he smiled.

Q put him down and he ran off to show the other children.

"Cute kid," I said. "What's his name?"

"His name is Peace."

"Well, Peace is a handsome little guy…I hope you're teaching him how to treat ladies a whole lot better than you do."

Q folded his arms and smiled, showing off that dimpled grin. "What'chu talkin' about now?"

"I'm talking about how you called me all types of bitches that night in the club."

Q's eyes narrowed a little, making his ass look even sexier.

"Where can I setup my camera equipment?" I asked, before he could say something smart. Knowing him, a remark was right on the tip of his tongue. I grew weak in the knees when I imagined being on the tip of his tongue, too.

"You can set up where ever you want, but the cabanas would probably be better for you."

I thought about the natural lighting effect it would give me. "The cabanas *would* be ideal," I agreed.

"Here, I'll carry this over for you."

My eyes grew big when I realized he had a pool. He must have been the only nigga in this hood that had one. Q took the equipment bags from me and carried them over to the cabana. Containing my surprise, I followed him and took in everything around me. All of the children looked so happy. One thing was for certain; Q loved the kids.

After helping me set up, Q left me to my work. I was surprised at how easy it was to find inspiration at a child's birthday party. I took some awesome shots of Peace playing with the animals, playing in the pool, and just interacting with the other kids naturally.

Surprisingly, I ended up having a lot fun, and instead of it feeling like work, it felt more like a hobby to me. In spite of my initial reservations, I was really happy that I'd agreed to doing the shoot. It was just what I needed to refuel that creative passion in me. Oftentimes, when I didn't get booked, I let that easily discourage me., and I would feel like giving up and giving into my father and Freddy's demands on my life. Luckily, I was once again inspired, and I had some excellent additions to my portfolio.

Every so often a kid would wander over and ask how my camera worked. I enjoyed explaining the mechanics to anyone that would listen. In between taking shots and helping kids stuff Now and Laters into pickles, I caught Q staring in my direction. I'd always give a small grin whenever our eyes made contact. It made me feel so giddy to bashfully smile at him, like some schoolboy crush. He was so handsome. I'd even taken some candid shots of him when he wasn't looking and he looked like he was straight from the pages of a high fashion spread.

I was just about to finally break the ice when a pretty light-skinned chick walked up to him. Judging by the way she was smiling and touching all over him as she spoke, I knew that the bitch wasn't a relative. Jealousy consumed me and I hated her ass without even knowing her name. Something told me they fucked around with each other, and that I probably didn't stand a chance. Not against a girl that looked like that anyway.

24

Q

"She wanted me to tame her feisty ass."

—*Q*

I was shocked that Mimi had taken it upon herself to come to my son's party uninvited. Sure, we fucked every now and then, and she stored work for me, but that didn't mean she could pull up whenever she wanted. Mixing business and pleasure clearly had Mimi thinking she was my bitch. However, she was sadly mistaken. Clearly, I gave the bitch too much credit for thinking she understood the dynamic of our relationship, or lack thereof.

"Damn, Q. You got me stalking your ass and shit just to see you. I thought we were gon' kick it once you got back to the city."

"When the fuck did I say that?? And since when do you show up to my crib unannounced? We ain't on that type of time, shorty."

"So, I ain't invited to my future step-son's birthday party?"

"Oh, so now he yo future step-son?"

"Damn right. You know how much Peace loves me!"

"That ain't what he says."

"And what does he say?" she asked, curiously.

"That yo ass will say anything," I laughed.

She grabbed my arm in a flirtatious way. "And I'll do anything, too." She licked her lips. "So, what's up with the after party?"

I don't know why, but I looked over at Sade. Our eyes locked briefly before she quickly looked away. I wasn't really in the mood for Mimi's bullshit right now. The bitch had just showed up out of the blue, like she wanted the dick right now, but I wanted something else...or better yet, someone else.

Breaking away from Mimi, I walked over to Sade when I noticed her packing up her camera equipment. "You leaving already?" I asked, not hiding the disappointment in my tone.

"Yeah, it's getting late. I'd better get back on my side of town. Plus, the deal was only for 2 hours. I'll print the photos and drop them off tomorrow."

She was going a mile a minute, and it was obvious she felt some type of way. "A'ight, cool. At least let me pay you for your time." I dug in my pocket for the cash and she quickly stopped me.

"Nah. Don't worry about it. Consider it restitution for that ride you gave me."

"Sade—"

"Can I use your bathroom before I leave," she interrupted.

"Uh, yeah...let me show you where it is." I led her into the house and directed her to the room down the hall. This was my second crib, and the one I used to host big events, like cookouts, and special occasions. I didn't want everyone in the hood knowing where I laid my head. As a boss, I had to move smart.

A few minutes later, Sade emerged from the bathroom. She tried to walk past me to leave but I quickly blocked her path. "Everything good with you? Why you leaving? You looked like you were having a good time."

"Yeah, well, it looked like you were having a good time, too." Her cheeks flushed in embarrassment the second it came out her mouth. Humiliated, she tried to walk around me again.

I grabbed and slammed her lil' ass against the wall, and before she could argue with me, I kissed her.

"Q—"

"Shut the fuck up. You talk too much. That's yo problem."

Shedding her will, she crushed her lips against mine. She could longer suppress her attraction, and neither could I. Grabbing her waist, I pulled her into me. I kissed her firmly and deeply, parting her lips with my tongue. I don't be just kissing everybody, I'd never even kissed Mimi but for some reason, with Sade, I loved it and wanted more.

When we kissed, it was like everything became quiet. Like she'd somehow stolen my last breath and showed me every other kiss I had was wrong. Grabbing my face, she deepened it, melting into me with desperate need. Like she wanted me to tame her feisty ass, and tame her I would.

I pushed her back against the wall, and grabbed one of her large breasts. A high-pitched moan escaped as her breathing rapidly increased. Burying my face in her neck, I slid my hands up her dress—

Suddenly, my phone started buzzing.

If it hadn't already ruined the mood, I would've gladly ignored it. Sade looked embarrassed as I glanced at the caller ID. "I gotta take this," I said, recognizing the number almost immediately. It was Camari's dumb ass calling collect from County Jail.

"It's okay. I should be going anyway," Sade said, scurrying off before I could stop her.

She really left without saying goodbye, I thought. *This broad ain't got no manners. She damn sure needed taming.*

After accepting the charges, I waited to be connected to Camari. "Q? Q! Thank God!" she said, relieved. "You don't know how grateful I am for you right now!"

"I don't know why. I ain't done shit yet...and after what you pulled in Oakland, I probably won't."

"But Q, you don't understand—"

"Your son turned three today, and where you at right now? In a muthafuckin' jail cell. I always said your priorities were fucked up. But this shit right here takes the cake."

"Look, nigga, don't try to pass judgment on me! You're no fucking better, you drug dealing piece of shit!"

"Man, get the fuck off my line, bitch—"

"No, no! Q, wait! I'm sorry, baby! I'm sorry! Please don't hang up." She sniffled. "You're the only person that can help me right now. Romello ain't accepting my phone calls. Please, baby. I have no one!"

"So, the nigga ain't bailing you out?"

"*Romello*? *Bail me out*? Please, yeah, right. He ain't even bail his own nigga out, who shot up the club *on his behalf*! I swear, that muthafucka is such a tightwad when it comes to certain shit!"

"So, lemme get this right? He can afford to pay hospital bills, but can't afford to bail his bitch out? That shit don't even sound right. Matter fact, I'm done even listening." I was about to hang up when she stopped me.

"Q, please! I'm serious! I'm telling you the truth! For God's sake! Have some heart, nigga! I'm your baby mama!"

"You ain't no fucking mom. Hell, you ain't even a woman."

"Q, please! Don't leave me in here with these hoes! These the same bitches I used to work the Blade with! Them bitches already don't like me, Q! I'm afraid! I'm afraid for my life! If I stay in here another night, these hoes will slit my throat in my sleep!"

"I'm sure it'd be well-deserved."

"Q, please!" she begged. "So, you telling me you can't bail me out???"

"I can..."

Camari sighed in relief. "Oh, thank god!" She exhaled

"But it ain't gon' be today." And with that, I hung up on her silly, simple-minded ass and went back to our son's party.

***

Later that night, I decided to call Sade and tell her ass about herself. She answered the phone on the third ring and patiently waited for me to speak. "You left without saying goodbye," I told her.

"I'm sorry...it's just...you seemed preoccupied, at the time."

"Well, I'm free now. Wassup?"

Sade gave a nervous laugh. "What'chu mean wassup?" she asked.

I appreciated the fact that she was a good girl, but that innocent act was starting to get stale. Besides, we both knew she wasn't as innocent as she liked to put on. "C'mon now. You know I'm feelin' you. I wouldn't have hit you up if I wasn't."

"Well, from what I see, a lot of women are feeling you. Or feeling on you," she smartly replied.

"We ain't talking about other women right now. We're talking about you. Let me take you out. What'chu got planned for this weekend?"

Sade hesitated.

"Look, gimme a chance, a'ight. I really wanna make this shit work. This is new to me. I don't really do shit like this." I added trying to break her down before she could say no.

Sade faltered with a response. "Um...I don't know, Q"

Suddenly, I grew agitated and just threw the fucking towel in. "You know what, never mind. Fuck it then. Just forget I even called yo stuck up ass." I disconnected the call and told myself that I was done with it. I couldn't keep chasing a bitch that obviously didn't want to be caught. So instead of waiting for her to come around, I called up Mimi and told her I was on my way.

25

Romello

"A wise pimp once told me, never trip on a bitch that's behind you."

—*Romello*

Sitting in my home theater, nursing a bottle of Henny, I knew that my next move had to be my best move. My two bottom bitches had been locked up. Fucking dumb ass broads. I always knew that Camari was reckless, but smashing into the back of the cop car had to be the dumbest shit she'd ever done. Right now, she and Chelsie were just being held on DUI, reckless endangerment, resisting arrest, and drug charges.

Luckily, Chelsie ditched the gun Camari used to kill Paul down a drainage ditch they crashed near, otherwise those bitches would've been facing the death penalty. Oh fucking well. A wise pimp once told me, never trip on a bitch that's behind you. And right now, Camari was definitely behind me. Yeah, she was my bottom bitch, and she brought me great money, but pussy was pussy. And there was definitely nothing special about hers. One hoe wasn't gonna stop my show. As fucked up as it sounded, she and Chelsie were on their own.

Suddenly, Naytoma strutted into the theater and immediately got down on her knees. Without saying a word or needing instruction, she pulled my dick out and began to alternate between deep-throating my shit and jacking me off with her small soft hands. I instantly felt my tension melting away as the head of my dick tapped the back of her throat repeatedly, causing her to gag.

"Fuck, suck this dick, bitch," I grunted as I began to thrust my hips upward into Naytoma's warm wet mouth.

Her eyes started to water and I felt her gag reflex every time I lifted my eyes. Wasn't nothing better than a pretty white bitch on her knees crying on your dick. After a few more minutes of harshly fucking her face, I felt my nut rising. Naytoma quickly whipped my dick out of her mouth and fell back on her feet as she swallowed my kids down her throat.

"Go get yaself cleaned up," I told her after I put my soft dick away.

I definitely needed that stress reliever. Especially since I had a big meeting with an important producer later today. Soren was the hottest producer out right now; his name rang big bells all throughout Hollywood and LA. He had come to my show, but that weak ass nigga Q had fucked up my chance to impress him. The club got shot up before Soren had the chance to see me do my thing. But with the money that Camari had secured from robbing her bum ass baby daddy, I was able to convince Soren's label that I'd be able to put my own money up to front the cost of producing my first album, as collateral. Just thinking about locking down this deal was making my dick hard all over again. I was gonna be up there with the likes of Snoop, and Dre. Nothing was gonna stop me from getting to the top of this rap game. Even if that meant breaking a few backs along the way.

***

I was sitting in the lobby of Soren's office waiting on him to arrive for our meeting. I looked around his office and admired his expansive mahogany desk, and the platinum accents he had around it. Framed gold records, as well of pictures of him with countless celebrities, musicians, and models lined the walls. This nigga was living the life I was destined to lead.

"Romello, how are you? Sorry for the wait," he said as he came in and shook my hand before taking a seat behind his desk.

"I'm good, I'm good." I replied. "I'm trying to get on your level." I said, waving my arm around his office.

"Well, from what I'm hearing, it's definitely possible," he smiled. "We heard the tracks that you sent over, and I definitely think that we could make some hot records together."

"Most definitely." I said as I rubbed my hands together. Just thinking about my rap career taking off made my palms twitch.

"With your looks, you can bring in the ladies and your flow and street knowledge can bring in the male audience," he said laying out the label's strategy. I nodded my head in agreement. "Now tell me about your background. What led you to a career in rap?" he asked me as he leaned back in his chair and folded his arms behind his head.

Ah, you know. I dabbled in the streets here and there, but women have always been my passion. I'm a ladies' man, what can I say." I said as I shrugged my shoulders and grinned.

"And do those ladies include the ones I saw in the club kissing your feet?" He asked.

"Oh, most definitely. Those ladies are special to me," I said giving him a pointed look. I couldn't come right out and say that I was their pimp. I didn't know if this nigga was a narc, or if he was phishing for information.

"What about the dark skinned one? Is she special?" He asked raising a brow.

"Oh, she's something special, alright," I said letting him know that I definitely caught his drift.

"Then I think this is going to be the start of a beautiful working relationship," he said as he extended his hand over his desk at me. I gave his hand a firm shake to seal this deal. If I had to sell Camari's soul to ensure my own success, then hey, that's just the way it is. Now I just had to get the bitch out of jail.

26

Camari

"I would gladly sacrifice myself if it meant that Romello could achieve his dreams."

—*Camari*

"This bitch always thought she was better than some damn body." I couldn't believe that I was in this position.

The night I got arrested, I watched as Romello sped off after realizing that the car we hit was a squad car. I knew better than to expect him to bail me out of jail, but it didn't stop me from at least trying to call him, of course, he never accepted any of them. It pained my heart to know that Daddy had abandoned me, especially after I secured the bag that I knew was necessary to put him on the map. But it was all for the greater good. I would gladly sacrifice myself if it meant that Romello could achieve his dreams. I meant it when I said he was my beginning, middle, and end.

"I know you heard me, you black ass bitch!" my fellow inmate screamed into my face, pulling me from my thoughts.

Ironically, it was the same bitch that I skirted off on the night I got arrested. She must have been picked up off the Blade by 12 that same night because she came in after me. This had to be rock bottom. I was in jail, surrounded by women that I literally spit on when I was riding high. Withdrawal had started to set in and I was in agonizing pain. Not to mention the humiliating treatment from the corrections officers. Out here, officers had no problem penetrating you during a strip search, or down right forcing you to suck their dicks if they felt like they could get away with it. "

Oh, this bitch is mute, huh?" My tormenter said looking at her accomplice. "I think we should put something in her mouth, give her a reason to be so quiet." Thing One said to Thing Two.

Just as one of them was about to force me into their smelly crotches, a guard came and banged his night stick on the bars of the cell. "That's enough you fucking dykes!" he barked. "Munch carpet on the Blade you flea ridden bitches. Jones, let's go."

"Me?" I asked in shock. "What did I do?"

"You're getting out," he said dryly.

I wanted to jump for fucking joy when I heard that shit. I guess Q came through for me after all. I made a mental note to give him some bomb ass head as a thank you. After what seemed like hours I was finally processed and able to walk through the doors of the county jail to freedom. I was shocked to see Romello standing against his candy paint Maserati waiting on me to come out.

"Daddy, you saved me!" I said running up to him and jumping into his arms. Despite the fact that he had seemingly abandoned me, all was easily forgiven when I laid eyes on him.

"Of course, I did. You my bottom bitch and we gotta get back to this money, baby." He said as he kissed me nastily, while roughly groping my fat ass.

"Anything for you, Daddy," I said as he placed me down on my feet. We got into the car and began the drive home. "Did you get Chelsie out too?" I asked as we rode down the freeway towards our condo.

WHAP!

Romello backhanded me so hard that I flew into the window of my door. "Bitch what have I told you about questioning me?" He asked in a calm voice.

"I'm sorry, Daddy." I said as I rubbed the knot that was forming on my forehead from the impact.

"I got a John lined up for you." he told me.

"Yes, Romello." I obediently replied.

"And don't fuck this one up," he warned. "The producer from West Coast Records apparently has a thing for crack whores, and you my darling fit the bill," he informed me.

I let his not so subtle insults roll off my back, as I thought about what he was saying. Evidently, I wasn't done sacrificing for Romello's career.

27

Jayda

"Two could play this game."

—*Jayda*

I was chilling at the crib, watching *Friends* and eating Turtles, when I suddenly heard a knock at the front door. Climbing off the sofa, I padded barefoot to the door to see who it was. My pussy leapt with joy once I saw that it was Shadow. After our last rendezvous, he had me feening for his ass. He never came through the night we talked on the phone, and now I was having withdrawals.

I quickly opened the door for him, only to be greeted with attitude. "Damn. Fuck I gotta keep knocking at the door for and shit. When ya'll muthafuckas gonna gimme a gotdamn key?"

"When your muthafuckin' ass start paying some gotdamn bills around here."

"Shit, say no more. Fuck you think a nigga here for?" Shadow pushed a wad of cash in my hands and invited himself inside. "Where my sister at?"

"She did a shoot yesterday and went to drop off the photos."

"Where 'bout?"

"Compton."

Shadow made a face. "Fuck she know in Compton?"

"Nigga, that's ya'll hood. You tell me."

"Whatever, man." He grabbed my ass roughly and pulled me close to him. "We got the whole crib to ourselves. That's what's more important." He tried to tongue kiss me but his phone started ringing.

"You gone get that?" I asked him.

Shadow looked at his phone. "Nah..."

He went to kiss me again, but it continued to ring incessantly. The person calling was obviously determined to get through to him.

"You sure you don't wanna get that?"

"Fuck this phone. I wanna get in them guts."

"Yo ass don't wanna get it 'cuz it's Tia, nigga!" I snatched the phone and looked at his caller ID, and sure enough, her name was there, flashing across his screen clear as day.

"Hold up, bitch!" Shadow lunged for his phone. "Hold the fuck up, muthafucka! Now yo ass getting outlandish! Gimme my shit 'fore I break yo fucking fingers!"

"Nah, muthafucka, you a liar! You said you and her weren't rocking like that, but yet here she is calling you! Are you with the bitch or not? And don't stand in my face and lie to me!"

"Man, just cuz that bitch hitting my line don't mean a muthafuckin' thing!"

"If it don't mean shit, answer the phone!"

"Nah, I ain't finna do all that. I ain't got nothing to prove."

I mugged him in his face. "Bitch nigga, you don't want me to know you still fucking her, stupid! But I guess I'm stupid too, 'cuz I actually believed your lying ass!"

Shadow grabbed my arm and slammed me up against the wall. "Hold up, bitch! I don't give a fuck who you are! Don't put your hands in my face unless you ready to lose them bitches!"

"Get your trifling ass out my face, you lying ass bitch! Matter fact, get the fuck out my house!"

"Trust me, I'm finna slide anyway. Your muthafuckin ass acting too crazy for me, and honestly, I don't wanna be around it. I stay here a second longer, you gon' fuck around and make me hurt you."

"You already hurt me, nigga!" I shouted trying my damnedest to hold in the tears.

"Ain't no sense in sticking around," he said, heading for the door.

"Good! Take your black ass back to Tia's! She the only one that wants your lying ass!"

"Fuck you, trash bag! Fat ass bitch! That's exactly where I'm going."

"Fuck you, broke ass convict! And take this chump change with you, bitch! Tia probably needs it more than me! Fucking broke ass project bitch aint got shit but yo' bum ass anyway!!" I yelled as I threw the wad of cash back at him. He let it fall to the floor as he roughly slammed the door behind him.

Seeking attention to make me feel better, I called LaMar and prayed that he'd answer, because right now, I didn't want to be alone. Plus, I needed to show Shadow's ass that 2 could play this game.

Much to my relief, he picked up on the 2nd ring. When I said that I wanted to see him, he told me to pull up.

***

I pulled up to LaMar's crib, playing Toni Braxton's *"Just Be A Man About It"*. This bitch was singing my life right now, and it was only propelling me more towards hating Shadow's ass and wanting to hurt him the way he was always hurting me. Even though we couldn't be together the way we wanted to, I still loved Shadow with every fiber of my being.

Just because I couldn't shout that shit from the roof tops, didn't make it any less real. And Shadow treated my love like it was disposable. Always waving that other bitch in my face, putting his hands on me, talking to me like I was nothing. I was fed up. Just as I was about to put my car in reverse and go home and sulk over my man, R. Kelly's *"When a Woman's Fed Up"* came up next on the CD I'd burned.

It's a fucking sign from Jesus himself, I thought.

With newfound determination, I got out of the car and went up to LaMar's door to knock, but before I could even raise my fist, he snatched the door open and roughly grabbed my arm yanking me inside.

Wasting no time, he kicked the door closed and threw me against it, kissing me hungrily and passionately. A moan forced its way from my lips as he trailed kisses down my neck and onto the tops of my breast that were threatening to spill out of the little camisole top I was wearing. LaMar wasted no time pulling them from my bra, and began alternating between licking my nipples and pinching them roughly. I rubbed the top of his head in anticipation, as he kept trailing kisses down my body.

He reached my skirt and roughly pulled it down my thick thighs. As I lifted my leg to discard my it, LaMar caught me by surprise and lifted my right one by the calf and placed it over his shoulder. He began to aggressively lick and suck on the crotch of my black lace panties, making me tremble violently like a leaf in hurricane and moan like someone was murdering me. The sensation of the lace material against my sensitive clit, and him pressing his warm wet tongue against it was overloading my senses and before I even knew what hit me, an orgasm so powerful ripped through me that I damn near collapsed. LaMar could barely hold my big ass up, I was struggling that hard.

"Damn girl, we ain't even get to the good part yet." He cheesed up at me, his face glistening with my cum. "Well show me then." I countered after I'd finally regained some of my composure.

"Say no more," he responded as he grabbed my arm and in one swift motion, pulled me down to the floor with him and got behind me.

I instinctively arched my back, and lowered the front of my body down, while I waited on him to get a condom in place. After strapping up, I felt LaMar's big hand grip my slim waist, as he used my hip for leverage and plunged himself inside of my tight, wet walls.

"*Ahhh!*" I bellowed out from the impact of his dick hitting the bottom of my pussy.

"Damn," I heard him mumble from behind me. He quickly caught a stride and began to slam into me with such force I felt rug burn forming on my knees and elbows. The sound of his balls slapping into my ass bounced off the walls and that shit was driving me wild.

"Fucking phat ass pussy," he growled as he picked up his right leg and really went ham on me.

"Oh shit, fuck this pussy baby!" I cried out, giving him extra motivation, as I felt myself nearing my peak.

I dug my nails deep into his lush carpeting as I felt my second orgasm rip through me. LaMar felt my walls clamping down on him and pulled out slowly and rammed back into me quickly. When he did that, I felt my juices squirt, covering our thighs, and dripping down onto the carpet. I felt him explode into the condom right after. He pulled out of me slowly, breathing like he'd run a 50-yard sprint. I rolled over onto my back and stared at him in amazement. This nigga made me squirt. I thought Shadow would be the only one who could make me do that.

"Why you looking at me like you seen the fucking boogeyman," he asked with a big cheesy grin.

"Nigga ain't nobody looking at you," I shot back as I brought my knees to my chest.

"Nah, you giving me that face bitches be giving a nigga when they done fell in love with the dick."

"Ha!" I laughed loudly.

"Ain't nobody gonna fall in love with yo' cocky ass." I told him.

"You're not a very good gambler. You already lost one bet to me." He said as he held his hand out to help me up off the floor. "Come on, let's go take a shower. Let me wash that fat ass off." He said, slapping me hard on the ass and watching it jiggle. Maybe falling in love with LaMar wouldn't be such a bad thing, though.

28

Sade

"I don't chase no bitch."

—*Q*

It had been three days since the party and I was sitting parked down the street from Q's house about to drop off the photos that I shot at his son's party. I'd came by the other day, but he wasn't around, so I figured I'd try again today.

I was still pretty raw from the way that he hung up in my face. To say I was offended would be an understatement. But I had to put all of that aside and be professional. I had done the job and now I needed to complete it. I just had to figure out a way of doing it without seeing Q. I finally gathered enough courage to get out of the car and make my way up to the door. I figured I could just put the prints in the mailbox and hightail it back to my car and not show my face.

Of course, I had no such luck because just as I was opening the mailbox, Q slung the door open with a scowl on his face. "Fuck you doing lurking around my crib for?" he asked me with a menacing glare.

"I just came to drop the prints from the party off," I said, as I placed them in the mailbox and closed it. "Now that that's done, I'll gladly be on my way," I said, catching an attitude turning on my heels to head back to my car.

"Man, you and that smart fucking mouth!" he barked at me. "Bring yo' simple ass in here." he growled lowly at me. I didn't know whether to be scared or turned on, but I obediently followed him into his palatial home.

"Look, Q, I—"

"No, you look," he said getting all in my personal space, once we crossed the threshold of the door. "I don't know why, but I fucks with your lil' mean ass and I'm tired of you giving me the fucking brush off." He said walking up on me.

My heart rate picked up and my adrenaline shot through the roof. Here I was in this dangerous man's house and he was all in my grill. I was so turned on, that I just knew my panties were soaking through my jeans.

"I'm not about to keep chasing you. I don't chase no bitch, so that should let you know how serious I am about this situation. Now I'm gonna ask you for the last fucking time. What are you doing this weekend? Nigga wanna take you out, and I ain't taking no for an answer."

By this time, my back was against the wall and Q put his arm up near my head to keep me from running off. I craned my neck, so that I could look up into his brooding face, as he towered over me. His manly cologne invaded my nostrils and I started to feel drunk off of his presence. His unwavering stare made me uneasy as he waited for an answer.

"If I have to ask again, it's gone be some fucking problems." He warned me in a low tone.

I finally found my voice. "I'm free this weekend," I said looking up at him in a lovesick stupor. He bent down and gently kissed me on my lips, leaving me breathless.

"That's what the fuck I thought. I'll pick you up tomorrow at 8, so your muthafuckin' ass better be ready.

And I don't just mean for the date. I mean the whole package," he said, gently pushing me towards the door.

"But you don't…" He gave me a look that instantly caused me to shut up. "Rrright, my mouth." I stuttered.

"Now go home and get ready for our date," he told me as he shut the door. I sat in my car for a few minutes in a daze. How the fuck did this nigga know where I lived?

***

The next night, I was standing in front of my bedroom mirror trying to figure out what to wear. "Bitch, why are you making this shit so damn hard?" Jayda asked in exasperation, falling back onto my bed. "Bitch, he didn't tell me where the fuck we're going! What if I wear the wrong thing, what if I'm over dressed, or underdressed."

"Bitch just go naked…Ya'll gone wind up fucking any damn way," Jayda said waving her hand at me.

"No. We're not and you already know why," I said giving her a knowing look before turning my attention back to the gray floor length dress I was holding up to my body.

"I know Q is your childhood crush and all, and that you're excited, but you should probably tell him upfront that you're holding your V card, Sade."

"Ugh...bitch why would you say that?" I whined.

I didn't need Jayda reminding me that I was a damn near 21-year old virgin.

"I'm just saying," she started. "You're gonna get your little virgin feelings hurt when he realizes you're not planning on giving up the goods, and he runs for the hills."

I glared at her through squinted eyes, as I listened to her lay out the truth. "And you know I'm not saying that to be a shady bitch, but I'm just warning you." Jayda was right, I knew her intentions weren't malicious, but that didn't make the truth sting any less.

"Of course, I know you're right, but is it wrong for me to be curious?" I asked her. "I mean, he's fine as hell, he's clearly paid, and under that rough ass thug exterior, he seems like he has a good heart." I reasoned. I don't even know why I was saying what I was saying, I was just making myself fall harder for a guy who inevitably wouldn't want me.

"I'm not saying don't go on the date. I'm just saying be honest. And if he's anything like LaMar, which I know he is, then you gone be sprung off the dick once you get it!" Jayda said referring to this fling that she had started up with LaMar.

"You're right, I'm gonna tell him. At some point. And you can keep those LaMar details to yourself!" I said as I tossed a stuffed animal from my dresser at her head, and laughed. After Jayda's pep talk, I put my nagging doubts out of my mind and finished preparing for my date.

At 8pm on the dot, I heard a knock at the door. Sure enough, Q was standing on the other side looking like a full course meal, with a side of biscuits. Bottom line is the nigga looked good enough to eat. "Hey," I said shyly as I came out of my apartment and closed the door behind myself.

"You look good as fuck," he said as he took in my appearance from head to toe.

I decided to keep it simple since I still had no idea where we were going on this date. I chose a simple heather gray maxi dress. I wore black sandals, and silver bangles up both of my arms. "You don't look half bad yourself." I told him.

Q was dressed nicely in some black jeans, red Chucks and a red and gold 49ers jersey. Taking my hand, he led me down to his Viper and opened the door for me. "Wow" I exclaimed "I had no idea you could be so gentlemanly." I said as I blushed. "All this for me?"

"The night is young," he said as he climbed in on his side. We drove for about 20 minutes before we reached the multiplex.

"What are we gonna do here?" I asked as we pulled up to the theater.

"Fuck it look like, we bout to see a movie," he said. I knew that asshole persona was still lurking under there somewhere. We went into the theater and Q bought us two tickets to see Love Jones. I was so excited because I was dying to see this movie and Jayda refused to go with me because she said she "didn't do that sappy nigga love shit."

Q, however, was the last person I expected to be seeing this movie with. As we sat in the quiet dark theater,

Q kept stealing glances at me, making me bashfully look away. I could tell that he was trying really hard to be chivalrous on this date. And I appreciated his willingness to go slow with me. I just didn't know how long he'd be able to maintain.

After the movie, he took me to this quiet soul food restaurant and we had good conversation. I hated to admit that I was shocked to learn that he could even hold one without referring to me as a bitch or a hoe.

"So, tell me more about Peace." I said, taking a sip of my sweet tea. "He seems like such a happy bright child."

"Yeah, that lil nigga is cool," he said smiling at the thought of his son, he clearly brought him great joy.

"You seem like you really like kids." I said.

"Yeah man, I do. If I could, I would have a whole football team of kids. Besides Peace, I basically raised my little sister Kai, and she's 15 now."

I smiled warmly at him, "Well, she sounds great. And that girl I saw you with, was that Peace's mother?" I asked, trying not to seem too obvious that I was prying.

"Come on shorty. You wanna know some shit, just ask." he scoffed. "Me and that girl light as hell, Peace is dark skinned. What kinda fool you take me for?" He said as he placed his hand against his chest, feigning offense.

"Okay, maybe I already knew she wasn't his mother. But what's up with you and her?" I asked, searching his face.

"Mimi is just something I stick my dick in, nothing more and nothing less," he said. being truthful.

"I'm sorry, I shouldn't even care. I just don't want to be stepping on anybody's toes with our little date," I said as I placed my hand on my chin and looked at him longingly.

"Look, I ain't with all this relationship shit, but I can see that you're a good girl and you seem like you would be worth the effort. I'm willing to put that effort in, but you gotta cut a nigga some slack," he said, reaching across the table to stroke my free hand.

"I'm okay with that Q. Just don't have me out here looking stupid," I said earnestly.

Q smiled at me and I returned it, but my smile instantly faded when I looked up and saw Freddy coming towards us. I dropped Q's hand and stared bug eyed at my incredulous ex.

"Freddy, what are you doing here?" I asked him as he came and stood at the corner of our table. Q noticed the agitation in my voice and looked up at the intruder now standing to his right.

"Aye homie, you got a problem?" Q questioned with an angry scowl on his face. Not sensing that his life was gravely in danger, Freddy decided to act tough.

"Actually, we do. You seem to be having dinner with my girlfriend," he said with a smarmy grin on his face.

"Say word," Q said as he turned his attention on me.

"Freddy, get the fuck outta here, we are not together and you know it!" I yelled, standing up out of my seat. This uptight nigga had me fucked up if he thought he was about to try to put me on blast in front of Q.

"You heard the lady, patna, now get the fuck up outta here before you regret it." Q stated coolly.

"I always knew this was the kind of man you would go for, Sade. Gutter trash man, for a gutter trash bitch." Freddy spat.

WHAP!

Without warning, Q stood up from his chair, reached into his waist and cracked Freddy in the face with the butt of a gun that he had there. Blood immediately began to squirt from Freddy's nose as he fell to the floor screaming. "I swear, I said it was gone be some problems!" Q shouted as he began to kick Freddy while he curled up in a ball on the floor of the restaurant. "Poindexter ass niggas like you always tryna' test a real nigga's gangsta!" he said between kicking Freddy in his stomach and stomping on his back.

"Q stop! You're going to kill him!" I yelled as I tried to pull him off of Freddy.

"Fuck nigga deserves to die!" he shouted enraged.

By now, other patrons in the restaurant were looking on in fear. This may have been a nice restaurant, but nobody was gonna call the cops. I'm not even sure what Freddy was doing over here, or why he was in that part of town. He thought places like this were beneath him. If he wanted to walk away with just this ass whipping, he'd leave the cops out of it too.

"Q, come on, let's go!" I pleaded as I grabbed on his arm to lead him away from the scene. He was breathing hard and his clothes and shoes had flecks of Freddy's blood on them. I was almost positive I stepped on a tooth on my way out the door. We got in the car and Q slammed the door, clearly still angry with the whole situation.

"You got a lot of fucking nerve questioning me about bitches and it's a whole nigga walking up on us during dinner." He spoke in an icy tone.

"Q. I swear it's not even like that. I broke up with Freddy three months ago and he just won't leave me alone. I'm sorry about tonight." I said in desperation.

He grew silent and gripped the fuck outta the steering wheel as he maneuvered his lightning fast sports car through the traffic. I didn't know what to say, or how to feel, so I just turned to look out of the window. Once again, I was in the car with a crazed lunatic and I didn't know what he was about to do.

29

Q

"I was a heartless nigga."

—*Q*

Because I was ignoring every traffic law known to man, Sade and I made it back to my house in no time. I got out of the car without saying a word and she quickly followed behind me. I could feel the fear radiating off of her. I wasn't going to hurt Sade and I knew she was telling the truth about that lame ass nigga she used to fuck with. I definitely knew his type.

I sold guys like him keys of coke and they went home to their Stepford wives and pretended to be upstanding citizens. Arlo always said the biggest crooks wore suits. I entered my crib with Sade hot on my heels.

"Q, I'm sorry that our date was ruined, but you can just take me home and I won't—"

I shut her ass up by shoving my tongue down her throat. I could feel the apprehension leaving her body as she melted into mine, returning my kiss hungrily. I picked her up and began to carry her to my bedroom.

Once we reached my master suite, I tossed her down onto the bed and quickly removed my clothes. I approached Sade, as she lay in the middle of my California king sized bed. She was looking at me like a deer caught in headlights. Nah, fuck that shit. She was shedding this good girl act tonight.

I roughly grabbed her by her ankle and pulled her to the end of the bed with me. After pulling her dress over her head, she lay there cowering in her bra and panties. My mouth was watering so I dove head first between her legs. I didn't even bother to remove her panties all the way, I just pushed them to the side.

I began to vigorously lick and suck on her clit. Snaking my tongue from the hood of her clitoris all the way down to the opening of her pussy. She responded by arching her back and grabbing onto the ends of my braids. Sade tasted sweet, like a good girl should and her incoherent moans and mumblings were like music to my ears.

I wasn't eating these ran through hoes out that I normally fucked with, and I was surprised at how much I missed the act. I got lost in feasting on her wetness and before I knew it, Sade was calling out to the heavens as her juices exploded from her and ran into my mouth.

"Oh Shit, Q! I'm cummin'!" she managed to scream out. After allowing her to catch her breath for a minute, I sat up on my knees and began to lower myself down onto her.

Sade grabbed onto my biceps like she was holding on for dear life. I placed the head of my dick at her opening and attempted to push my way inside of her. When I was met with resistance, my eyes shot open in surprise. I felt Sade tense up, like she already knew what I was about to say.

"Yo, you a virgin?" I asked with distress in my voice. I don't know why, but this shit was really fucking with my head. I had literally never fucked a virgin before. Shit, my own baby mama was a damn street walker. I wouldn't even know what a virgin looked like. "I...I was gonna tell you, but everything happened at the restaurant and I just got caught up in the moment. I'm sorry Q. I'll just call a cab home," she said sadly, as she tried to sit up and get dressed.

"Hold up, hold up," I said pushing her back down. "Are you one of them 'save it till marriage bitches?" I asked.

"No, it's not that. I just never felt like I met a guy I wanted to sleep with...Until now." She said that like she was embarrassed.

"So, you saying you want me to be your first?" I asked her.

All of a sudden, I felt like my chest weighed one thousand pounds. I was a heartless nigga. I had more bodies under my gun, and more bitches under my belt than I could count, but the thought of Sade offering me something so precious seemed like a huge responsibility. One that I frankly didn't know if I was capable of handling. I sat up and looked her in the eyes.

Sade's face was a mixture of innocence, worry, and desire. But her demeanor calmed me. She wasn't out here trying to turn a trick, or hit a lick. She was just a regular around the way girl, trying to live her best life. It reminded me of why I named my son Peace. Maybe Sade would be just what I needed, especially when it was so many niggas trying to knock me off my spot. And if that's what the case was, then I was determined to try to be what she needed me to be.

Pushing my reservations to the side I placed my lips against hers. I'd never made love before, but I was willing to try for Sade. I positioned myself at her opening again and slowly eased my length into her. I had never felt anything like this before. Her walls were so tight and wet that it was almost painful.

Every time I moved my hips back, I could feel her pussy sucking me back in. This shit was amazing. I looked down and Sade's face was balled up like she was dying. She was being a trooper though and trying to take the dick like a big girl. I sped my thrusts up, knowing good and damn well that I wouldn't be able to last much longer.

"Oh, Q," she moaned breathlessly underneath me and when she did I lost all my fucking composure.

"Fuck, I'm cumming!" I shouted as I filled her up with my seeds. It just hit me that I never bothered to put a condom on. I rolled off of her and pulled her into my chest. I kissed the top of her forehead.

"You know that pussy mine now, right?" I asked her as she smiled at me while playing in my chest hairs.

"Of course," she replied.

That was all I needed to hear

30

LaMar

"When you find a real one, you'll know."

—*Arlo*

I was sitting on the porch at Q's crib listening to him try to make arrangements to bail Camari out of jail. I still hadn't gotten the money together that sheisty bitch took from us. The tension between me and Q was palpable and if something didn't give soon, I wouldn't be surprised if he tried to take me out.

"Fuck you mean she not there anymore? Where the fuck did she go?" he roared into the phone. "You fucking incompetent ass niggas, man!" He cursed as he threw his cordless phone in a fit of rage.

"What they say?" I asked him. Little did he know, I was just as concerned about Camari's whereabouts as he was.

"Man, they talking about she was already bailed out, but they wouldn't say by who. On blood, if it was that nigga Romello, I'm done with her ass fa real fa real," he seethed. "Look man..." Q started. "I'm done sulking about that bitch setting you up. Her ass can't be saved and I'm turning in my 'captain save a hoe' cape. From here on out, fuck that bitch, she's dead to me." He said stroking his goatee.

Clearly, this had been heavy on his mind. "Man, on God, I'm gonna pay you back, but we gotta let karma deal with that shiftless hoe." I told him. I kept to myself the fact that her karma would be coming from me. Quickly changing the subject I asked, "So what's up with you and homegirl from the club?"

"*Maaaannn...*" He said as a huge grin formed on his face. "She's a fa real good girl and that shit got my nose wide open," he replied as he looked off thinking about ole girl. "I'm so used to do-nothing ass bitches, like Camari, but baby girl got an education, and goals, and dreams. That shit is refreshing. Especially coming from where we come from."

"Real shit," I replied as we sparked up a blunt. "And her friend bad as fuck, too," I said as I passed the blunt back to him. "

Nigga you a fool!" he said as his laughter caused him to break into a fit of coughing. "What her friend got to do with her?" he asked still laughing.

"Man, you know the saying, 'birds with good pussy flock together,'" I said before cracking up.

"Nigga that's not the saying and yo' simple ass know it," he responded.

It felt good to sit back and kick it with my day one again. Shit didn't feel right when me and Q were out of whack. It was like I was missing my right foot or some shit. Yeah, I knew I was low down for fucking his baby mama in the first place, but after the way she did me I knew, I had to let whatever soft spot I had for that bitch harden the fuck up.

We spent a little more time chopping it up, before we saw Arlo, ambling down the street. He looked a little better than he usually did, like he'd found some new cleaner clothes and had maybe had a shower recently.

"Aye! What's happening young bloods?" he said as he raised his hands to us in greeting.

"Shit, you tell us, OG," I told him as he came up the stairs to the porch and dapped us up.

"I was hoping I would run into you two," he said as he pulled up another white plastic chair to sit in with us.

"Oh word?" Q asked as he passed him the blunt, and lit up another one. Arlo was a cool dude, but wasn't nobody smoking after his vagrant ass.

"Yeah, word on the street is that it was some jackin' ass Crips that shot up ya'lls trap last week. Some nigga named Dreeco was talking about how he had it out for you two for killing his cousin in the ambush. Nigga said they the ones that hit the other trap since they failed the first time. I don't know why they gunning for ya'll like that. They don't sound too bright. If they knock ya'll off, they clearly aren't ready to take your place," he laid out for us.

"Damn, that's some real shit," I said, taking in everything that he was saying. The name Dreeco sounded familiar. I knew that him and a couple other cats were some known jack boys out in Long Beach. LBC niggas wasn't shit, I tell ya.

"Yeah man," Arlo continued. "That's why you two have got to stick together. I done already told this nigga Q, but I'mma tell you too LaMar," Arlo said, turning to face me. "You can't do this street shit forever. You'll wind up just like me. Broke, homeless, lost ya family, lost ya kids."

"You ain't got no damn kids, Arlo," I said giving him the screw face.

"Lil' nigga, I wasn't always like this." he said. "I had three sons, by three different women. One was my wife, one was my mistress and one was a lil something I picked up off the Blade. By the time they were toddlers, I was already too far gone, gettin' high on my own supply. Just fucking up, man," he said as he looked off into the distance clearly traveling back down memory lane. "Being out here like this ain't never did nothin' for nobody. I just wish I could go back in time and change things, you know?" he said wistfully. "I wish I would have done better by my wife. That's what you young cats is missing," he started. "Ya'll think being single forever is the move, when what you really need is to find you a good girl, with a good head on her shoulders and do right by her."

"Man, Q done already beat you to that," I said, putting him on blast.

"Man, get the fuck on, ain't nobody settling down," he said grinning.

"Aw look, this nigga lying," Arlo said as he leaned into me while we shared a laugh at Q's expense. "That's what you say now, but when you find a real one, you'll know," He said, dropping some more wisdom on us and I soaked it all in like a sponge. Arlo may not have been perfect, but I wished that I had a male figure like him in my life when I was growing up. He had seen and done it all and that kind of wisdom was invaluable.

31

Shadow

"I wouldn't hesitate to kill over her."

—*Shadow*

Pacing back and forth in front of Dreeco, I wracked my brain trying to come up with a new attack plan. It had been about three weeks since we hit Q and LaMar's smaller trap, and the money we made was starting to dwindle. After tricking off on shopping sprees, new chains, and a new whip, we needed to re-up and fast.

I'd even broken Tia off with a little change to help her with her kids. And to top it off, Jayda not answering my calls was only adding to my growing stress. Regardless of what she thought, I really did love her ass, probably more than I loved myself. A nigga just had a fucked up way of showing it.

Even though my mother was an amazing woman, her death left me with some serious abandonment issues. In my eyes, all women were going to leave you eventually. Even the ones that loved you unconditionally.

"Man, will you sit yo' monkey ass down!" Dreeco shouted at me. "You making me nervous and when I get nervous, I start shooting," he threatened.

"Man, if we don't come up with something fast, shit is not gonna end well for us," I shouted back. "The longer we sit on our asses, the more time they have to figure out who hit them and come gunning for us."

"Man, I already told you, I been going to them whack ass jack off fests that nigga be having at the skate park. I'm this close to having the new routine down pat. And as soon as them niggas get comfortable, then we take them the fuck out." He said trying to explain his strategy. The only problem with that was I'm sure that nigga had been made by somebody. Yeah, he initially threw the heat off himself at the first meeting, but it was inevitable that Q and LaMar would eventually realize they fingered the wrong guy because the leaks hadn't stopped.

"Man, I'm too fucking stressed for all this shit," I said, throwing my hands up. I hopped in my new old school Chevy that I copped and sped towards Tia's house. When I got there, I hadn't even knocked good before she answered the door in nothing but a lace thong. She moved out of the way to let me in. I hoped she wasn't in a talking mood because I just wanted to bust this nut and relieve some damn stress.

Unfortunately, Tia wasn't picking up the vibe I was putting down because she immediately began to run her mouth about nonsense. What kinda bitch answered the door damn near naked, but started nagging rather than getting down to business? This was exactly why Tia could never hold a candle to Jayda.

Speaking of Jayda, I was brought back to the moment when I heard Tia mention her name. That didn't so much surprise me, seeing as how she was always taking pot shots at her. She always suspected that we were fucking around on the low and never missed an opportunity to try to prove she was better for me.

"Back up, what you just say?" I asked her.

"Ugh...my cousin's baby's daddy told me that she been seeing your sister's dark ass friend riding around in that nigga LaMar's drop top. I guess the bitch think she better than somebody since she snagged herself a wanna be baller," she said rolling her eyes in disgust.

"Fuck you mean Jayda been rolling around with that nigga LaMar?" I asked feeling my blood begin to boil.

"Yeah, Kendria told me that she seen them being real cozy and shit. Hitting the mall, going out to eat. I guess she finally found herself a man," she said giving me a gotcha grin. If she thought that she was claiming her stake as the number one bitch in my life, then she was sadly mistaken. All Tia did by divulging this information to me, was make me want Jayda even more.

"Aye, I gotta go," I said as I turned to head to the door and rush back to my car.

"I knew it!" Tia shouted as she jumped on my back and started pounding on it with her fists.

"Bitch, what the fuck is wrong with you?" I shouted as I tried to shake her ass off of me.

"You been fucking that black ass bitch behind my back all this time!" she screamed as she lost her grip on me and fell to the floor.

"What the fuck is you talking about?" I said, trying to play dumb.

"You think I don't know! Nigga, it's not as fucking secretive as you thought. Your sister is a real dumbass for never figuring it out," she said, crying uncontrollably.

"Don't you *ever* talk about my sister, do you hear me, you stupid bitch?!" I shouted into her face as I grabbed her off the floor by her hair.

"I fucking hate you Shadow! You ain't shit!" she screamed, trying to free her hair from my grip.

"Let me tell you something." I said getting in her face. "If you ever disrespect my girl, or my sister again, I will shoot you in the fucking head and leave your kids as orphans. Do you understand me?" I asked her menacingly. If she wanted to know about Jayda so bad, then she should know I wouldn't hesitate to kill over her.

"Y—yes," she stuttered as snot and tears ran down her face.

"Good," I said as I tossed her back down to the floor. I left out of her crib and jumped in my car with murder on my mind. I had gone to Tia's house to release my stress and wound up adding to it ten-fold. One thing was for certain, them niggas Q and LaMar had to go. *Especially* that nigga LaMar.

32

Sade

"Q made everything in my world right."

—Sade

Ever since the night I gave Q my virginity, we had been joined at the hip. Anytime that he didn't spend in the streets, or with Peace, he spent with me. We had quickly grown inseparable. Plus, I hadn't heard a peep out of Freddy since Q cracked his face open, and for that I was grateful. My life was going great.

Aside from the fact that I had to dodge a few phone calls from my dad, I couldn't be happier. Even my business had picked up. Bookings had been steadily coming in and it was all thanks to Q. We had gotten off to such a rocky start, but I couldn't be happier about the direction of our relationship. And don't even get me started on the sex. Although, I had nothing to compare it to, I was convinced that Q was hands down the best lover on the west coast, hell, probably even America.

I had just pulled up to his house so we could have a movie night with Kai and Peace. They were such good kids. Q had filled me in on the situation with Camari and it was amazing how well adjusted Peace was. Q did a good job of shielding him from his mother's evil ways. And Kai was an interesting girl. She reminded me a little bit of myself at that age, besides the whole lesbian tomboy thing. She was really artistic, and creative. She had a great knack for drawing and had even asked me to show her how to work my camera so that she could learn photography. I really enjoyed spending time with all four of us and was starting to fall in love with the kids, just as much as I was falling in love with Q.

Just as I was opening my door to get out of the car, I saw a call coming through from my daddy. It had been weeks since I was ducking him and I knew that I would have to talk to him eventually. I finally decided to face the music and answer the phone. I already knew what he was calling about.

"Hello?" I answered bracing myself for whatever lecture I was about to get.

"ARE YOU OUT OF YOUR DAMN MIND??" he bellowed into my ear.

I had to quickly pull the phone away from my face or I would have burst my damn ear drum. He didn't even give me a chance to respond before he continued his tirade.

"YOU HAD SOME DRUG DEALER BEAT UP FREDDY??" he shouted.

"What? Daddy no, that's not what—"

"SHUT UP!" He yelled, cutting me off. I stared at the phone like it had sprouted heads. My father was strict, and stern, but he had never talked to me like this. "DO YOU KNOW WHAT HIS FAMILY IS CAPABLE OF?" he continued to shout.

"Daddy, stop yelling at me!" I cried into the phone. I couldn't believe that my father was speaking to me this way.

"You think I care about your tears?! The Billups family was going to back my run for chief of police. And now thanks to you and whatever gangbanger you want to throw your life away for, it's all fucked to hell! My whole career, everything I've worked for. DOWN THE DRAIN" He barked.

"What does that have to do with me?" I shouted. "How am I capable of ruining your career?!" I screamed back at him. None of what he was saying made any sense.

"If you thought Freddy was with you because he loved you, then you're dumber than I thought you could be!" he sneered. "Your relationship was an arrangement between me and Freddy's father. But you just had to grow a fucking backbone and break up with him. You've never made smart choices. From your major in college, and clearly your taste in men, you've been nothing but a disappointment to me ever since your mother died. You and your deadbeat brother," he added.

Words couldn't describe the pain that my heart was in right now. My father's searing revelation cut through me like a hot knife through butter. I didn't even know how to respond to that, so I did the next best thing and just hung up the phone.

My father immediately called me back, but I simply turned the phone off and put it into my glove compartment. I had no idea what just happened. I mean, I knew my daddy would be upset about Q beating up Freddy, but I had no idea he would be this mad. And I certainly wasn't expecting him to tell me that he thought I was a disappointment to him. I didn't want to go into Q's house crying, so I sat there and composed myself in the car for ten minutes. I wouldn't give my father the satisfaction of stealing my joy.

***

Kai, Q, Peace, and I were sitting in Q's theater room watching *Friday* on VHS, and pigging out on snacks. I tried to hide the fact that I was upset, but Q kept asking me if something was wrong. I Just gave him small smiles to try and ease his mind.

I got up to get a refill on my drink and use the bathroom about halfway through the movie. After peeing, and flushing the toilet, I stood at the sink to wash my hands. I stared my reflection in the mirror and why wondered why my father couldn't just love me like a normal father.

It was bad enough growing up the daughter of a cop in fucking Gang Central, California. I always felt like I had a target on my back. Nobody trusted me, and friends came few and far between. And my father's strict and controlling behavior didn't help the situation any. And he only got worse after my mother was murdered. I splashed some cold water on my face to try and compose myself. "You can't steal my joy. You can't steal my joy." I chanted over and over to myself trying to quiet my swirling thoughts. I had no idea how to handle this situation.

All of a sudden, the bathroom door swung open as Q barged in, and shut it behind himself. "Why you walking around looking all sad and shit, huh?" He asked me as me turned me so my back was facing the mirror, and lifted me to sit on the edge of the sink.

"Baby, I promise, it's nothing," I said as he started to reach under my skirt and pull my panties down. "Q, what about the kids?" I giggled as he attacked my neck and collarbone with kisses.

"Man, fuck them kids," he joked as he pulled his dick out of his sweats that he was wearing. He lifted my legs, placing them in the crooks of his arm, and plunged into me in one deep motion. We'd only been having sex for a few weeks, and each time still felt like the first.

"*Aaahhh*," I screamed as I felt his girth stretching me to capacity. Q covered my mouth with his, as he expertly stroked my pussy.

"Shut the fuck up," he moaned into my mouth. The feeling of him stroking my g-spot over and over with his curved dick was almost too much for me to bear. I bit down on my lip so I wouldn't cry out too loud as he continued his attack on my pussy. "This my pussy, right?" he questioned me as he grabbed around my throat and started slowing his strokes down just a little.

"*Mmmm*, yes, Q. This is your fucking pussy, baby," I moaned in ecstasy.

"Betta be," he said kissing me sloppily but passionately. It was like Q could never get enough of kissing me, and that was just fine by me. "Oh shit, I'm finna bust." He cried out. Hearing his moans and knowing that I was pleasing him was such a turn on. I was so caught up on all of the emotions that I was feeling, my head felt like it was swimming.

Right as I began to ride the wave of the orgasm that was crashing over me, my mind went numb. "I love you!" I cried out before I could even stop myself. Right when I said those three word I could never take back, Q's body went rigid as I felt him shoot his load of warm cum deep inside of me.

We were both breathing hard, trying to recover from the quick yet intense fuck session. With my back pressed against the bathroom mirror, Q peeled his body off of mine, as I felt his limp dick sliding out of me. I was so embarrassed. I couldn't believe that I told him I loved him. And during sex no less! Now he was going to think that I was some naive little girl too dickmatized to see straight. I mean, yeah, I actually did love him. But I certainly hadn't planned on telling him that while he fucked me on his bathroom sink.

Once I was able to sit up straight, I kept my head down trying to avoid Q's face. He hooked my chin with his finger and forced me to look him in the eye. "I love you, too," he said before placing his lips on mine. Instantly, all of my pain from earlier vanished. Q made everything in my world right.

33

Q

"I made a promise to myself to never bring any harm Sade's way."

—*Q*

"Ewwwww, ya'll nasty!" Kai and Peace taunted as Sade and I walked back into my theater room.

"Man, ya'll little bastards nosey as fuck." I said throwing a pillow from the couch at them.

"Ya'll just nasty!" Kai taunted again.

"Yeah, a'ight. I'll be nasty until ya beggin' ass want some new Jordans." I responded.

"Okay, okay." she said raising her hands in mock surrender.

Sade had her face covered by her hands as she flushed in embarrassment. "Don't be acting all shy now," I scolded her. "I told ya loud ass to keep it down," I said as a pried her hands away from her face.

"Shut up Q!" she said as she gave me an icy stare. Clearly, this situation was not amusing to her.

"Come on ya'll, let's go get some ice cream or something," I offered. "It's too nice to be cooped up inside all day," I said as everybody began to stand and stretch to head to the car.

***

So far, being with Sade was proving to be one of the best decisions I'd ever made. She was so easy going and fun to be around, not to mention my son and little sister loved her. She wasn't after me to get in my pockets, or make a come up. She just genuinely liked to be around a nigga, which was new for me.

Once I broke her guard down, she really opened up to me. We would stay up all night cakin' on the phone on some simpin' ass 'you hang up' type shit. I didn't have to be so hard around her. It just felt right. That's why I wasn't surprised to hear her say that she loved me. I knew I didn't have much experience with love. Hell, the only bitch I ever loved set my best friend up and chucked the deuces up to our son. But this shit with Sade felt right, even though we were moving hella fast, I had no plans to slow it down. Arlo was right, you definitely knew when you found a real one.

We pulled up to the Dairy Queen around the corner from my crib and Sade picked Peace up so that she could read the menu to him. "And what do you think sounds best?" she asked him.

"Sunday!" he shouted, making Sade tickle him on his stomach. He burst into a fit of giggles.

Watching how easy it was for Sade to interact with Peace, just made me hate Camari so much more. I hadn't heard a peep from that bitch since she called me begging to bail her ass out of jail. I figured that bitch ass nigga Romello had done it, and if so, then Camari was officially his problem.

Me and Peace certainly didn't need her ass. Just as we finished ringing up our order, I spotted Arlo coming down the street. I was happy because he could finally meet Sade. I had told her all about Arlo, and how he was like a father to me. With the type of person that Sade was, I knew she wouldn't judge him because he was homeless.

"Arlo! I called out to him.

"Babe, I'm gonna go grab some napkins. I'll be right back." Sade said.

"Alright, hurry up. I want you to meet Arlo." I said to her as I grabbed her around the waist and pulled her in for a kiss.

"Nigga I'm going ten steps to the left, I'll be right back," she said as she laughed and pulled away from me.

"My nigga Q." Arlo said as he walked up to the table that we were sitting at. "You protecting ya' neck outchea?" he asked.

"Oh, you know my hittaz ain't far." I informed him.

LaMar and I had yet to corner the niggas who hit our trap. We were a lot closer after the information that Arlo had given us. We had taken most of them niggas out but a few were still slipping under our radar. And while it may have seemed like I let my guard down, I always had shooters posted in the cut. I just didn't want to alarm Sade and the kids. Although, I'm sure Kai was a little tougher than Sade. I laughed at that thought.

"What's so funny?" Arlo asked.

"Nothing man. I want you to meet somebody," I said just a Sade came walking back with the napkins. "Baby, this is Arlo, Arlo this is my real one." I said pulling her down into my lap as she blushed and cheesed at me.

"It's nice to meet you Arlo, I've heard so much about you." She said as she extended her hand for him to shake. See what I mean? Despite the fact that Arlo was dirty and tattered, Sade still greeted him with respect and humanity. The gesture wasn't lost on Arlo either. He grabbed her hand and went to kiss the back of it.

"Watch it ol' man" I warned him. "Don't get fucked up being fresh with my woman now," I jokingly threatened him.

Arlo raised his head and was about to respond to my jab when he suddenly looked like he'd seen a ghost. The little remaining color drained from his face and he dropped Sade's hand like it was burning him. Suddenly, he took off running.

Alarmed by his sudden change in demeanor, I called after him. "What the fuck, Arlo?" But he had already booked it down the street.

"Did I do something wrong?" Sade questioned, clearly hurt by Arlo's hot then cold reception of her.

"Nah, baby. He's an old drunk. You know they ain't right in the head."

***

The next day, I had just finished rounding on my traps. Since our hit, LaMar and I had been a little more hands-on than usual with our operation. It was an inconvenience as the boss to be bogged down in the little details, but at the end of the day the buck stopped with us, so the sacrifice had to be made. As I was walking back to my car, I spotted Arlo between two of the traps, looking like he was high as Cootie Brown.

"Man, Arlo you back on that shit?" I questioned, the disappointment evident in my tone.

"Q, you don't understand," he said as he burst into a fit of tears. "It was her. It was her," he said as he began to cry harder.

"It was who? Man, what the fuck are you talking about?" I asked growing agitated at him talking in circles.

"I done a lot of fucked up shit in my life man, a whole lot." He said. "But that woman didn't deserve that. That girl didn't deserve that." he said as he used the bottom of his once white t shirt to blow his nose.

"Who didn't deserve what? You betta quit talking in riddles and get to the fucking point, old man!" I shouted. In a minute, I was gonna blow his ass away just for wasting my time.

"Your girl, Sade," he said through more tears.

What the fuck did Sade have to do with this? I thought back to the other day when he ran off on us at the Dairy Queen. It was like realization washed over him when he looked in Sade's face. Whatever memory she brought back wasn't a pleasant one.

"Years ago, when I *really* hit rock bottom, I was out here snatching purses just looking for my next fix. One night, I ran up on this lady in the store. She had two kids with her. I just meant to take her purse man, I didn't mean to kill her!" He said as he began to sob even more violently.

"That girl. She was a little girl then, but that was definitely her," he said as he began to mumble incoherently to himself.

I finally began to understand what he was saying. Arlo had killed Sade's mama. "Nigga, what the fuck is you talking about? You killed my girl's mom?" I asked just to make sure I was hearing him right.

"I didn't mean to. I didn't mean to." He continued to cry.

"Damn man...That's fucked up."

POP!

POP!

I drew my gun from my waist and fired two shots into Arlo's chest. His revelation disturbed me to my core. Sade and I had talked about how negatively the death of her mother had affected her and that it had basically torn her family apart. It was something that we bonded over, the loss of a mother at a young age. Arlo had hurt my girl and I made a promise to myself to never bring any harm Sade's way. If that meant taking Arlo out, then that's just how it had to be.

34

Jayda

"I was just tired of sneaking around behind my best friend's back."

—*Jayda*

"Well, look who the cat dragged in," I said as Sade brought her sneaky ass through the door of our home.

"Bitch please, you ain't been here either so don't even try to do me." She laughed.

"Bitches get boyfriends and leave their friends in the dust." I fake pouted at her.

"Girl, you will be just fine," she sassed me with her hand on her hip.

I was seeing a whole new side of her ever since she'd gotten herself some dick. "But seriously, I'm glad to see you being so happy. Q is definitely a good look on you."

My friend had a glow about her that was radiating from within. She looked much happier than she did when she was with that square ass Freddy.

"*Ugh*," she sighed as she plopped down on the couch next to me. "He's so much more than I expected. He's damn near perfect. I mean, he's a great father, he's paid, he treats me with respect. Which is saying a lot considering how we met."

"Bitch you ain't neva lied," I responded. "So, are you helping him with the block party?" Every summer Q and LaMar would throw a big block party for the hood. They had bounce castles and games for the kids, endless food and drinks for everybody in attendance. All they asked for in return was for there to be no violence or nonsense. And for the most part, everyone obliged their generosity.

"Yeah, he even hired me as the official photographer. I swear, it's like he's more invested in my dreams than even I am. Every time I get discouraged or feel like I'm not booking enough or my shoot didn't turn out right, he sets me straight. And by sets me straight, I mean he curses my ass out and then fucks the shit out of me." I bust out laughing at her last statement. "Girl, I told you once you got the dick it would be curtains for you."

"And you were right!" she exclaimed as we slapped fives.

We spent the next few hours just catching up, watching reruns of The Real World and having girl talk. "I'm gonna go lay down for a little bit before I head back over to Q's house tonight."

"I see you girl, dick got you all tired and shit," I said teasingly.

She shot me a bird before she slammed the door to her bedroom. I was genuinely happy for my friend and secretly patting myself on the back. If I hadn't dragged Sade to Romello's doomed show, then her and Q might not have crossed paths. I was thinking of adding "matchmaker" to my resume.

As I surfed through the channels looking for something else to watch, my phone rang. Looking at the unknown number flash across my screen, I debated on whether or not to answer it. "Hello," I said as I picked up on the last ring.

"Fuck you doing? I need to see you," Shadow said, in an urgent tone.

"Well hello to you too, nigga. I'm fine, your sister is good. And how is your no good black ass?" I questioned him.

"Bitch, ain't nobody got time for your pissy ass attitude. I'm tryna pull up on you," he sneered, ignoring everything I just said.

"Well, you can't. Sade is home and I'm not in the mood for company," I said dryly.

It got quiet on the other end of the phone before he said, "And why the fuck is that?" I caught the hint of anger in his tone.

"Because I'm just not, Shadow. I'm tired of being your dirty little secret. You only come around when Tia doesn't want you. You can't keep your hands to yourself. And frankly, I deserve better," I said laying it all out there for him.

The time I had been spending with LaMar made me realize that my relationship with Shadow was severely one sided. I never saw him outside of my bedroom and honestly, I was just tired of sneaking around behind my best friend's back. If I couldn't keep it real with Sade, then I was failing as a friend, and she didn't deserve that. Sade was as thorough as they came and it was time that I started to reciprocate.

"Or is because you out here fucking with these weak ass niggas?" He barked into phone.

"What are you talking about?" I asked, playing dumb.

"Yeah, bitch, you thought I didn't know," he said, causing the hairs on my neck to stand up.

"I—I don't know what you're talking about nigga," I said trying to keep my voice from breaking and giving me away.

"A'ight bet." He snapped. "I hope getting caught in the crossfire is worth it dumb ass trick," he threatened before hanging up in my face.

I sat there stunned for a moment before calling LaMar. I didn't take Sharif's threats lightly and I had to warn my man.

35

Shadow

I couldn't catch a break with these fucking bitches man. First Jayda, then Tia, now Jayda again. To know that my bitch was sleeping with the enemy was like the ultimate blow to my ego. I broke Jayda in and she was always supposed to be mine. No other man was supposed to get a taste of my pussy. And to know that the same nigga that I had been gunning for was disrespecting me in such a way was unacceptable.

I had gathered the rest of my crew, or what was left of it. Q and LaMar had caught up with a few of my goons and taken them out, but Dreeco and I were untouchable. They still hadn't caught up to me yet, and I was banking on them still slipping. My niggas were shook and quickly losing faith in my ability to lead them, but I had a plan that was gonna put us right where I needed to be. I just hoped Jayda didn't have to be a casualty of this gang shit.

36

Camari

"My spirit was broken and I was starting to lose my mind."

—*Camari*

After bailing me out of jail, Romello took me home, got me cleaned up, got me a fix and then informed me that we were going to a meeting with the big wig producer that was going to be working on his debut album. He'd finally signed a record contract and had been working tirelessly in the studio so that he could push it out before the end of the summer. What he neglected to mention was that there was an unwritten clause in the contract virtually selling me to Soren, his producer.

For the past month, I had been literally chained to a post in the corner of Soren's basement where he would torture me sexually whenever he felt like it. These Hollywood types always had weird fetishes and derelict sexual desires that their skinny white wives wouldn't fulfill.

So whenever he got the urge, Soren would spend hours pissing on me, fucking me in the ass roughly with no lube, making me suck his dick until I threw up, he'd even begun to get off on making me eat my own vomit.

I kept trying to tell myself that it was all for the greater good, that I was doing this because Romello needed me. I was helping him to be successful in life, and he in turn would reward my loyalty in some way. But I was starting to see how wrong that line of thinking really was. Romello had promised that he would come back for me once his album was finished. He told me it would only take two weeks, since he already had the tracks written, and they just needed to be recorded. But two weeks turned into three, three turned into four and I was beginning to lose track of time. Soren only fed me enough to keep me alive and gave me enough drugs to keep the shakes off me. I could feel myself dying. My spirit was broken and I was starting to lose my mind.

I heard the door to the basement open and like a dog salivating at the sound of the dinner bell, my body began to quake in fear. I used to enjoy the painful pleasure that Romello would inflict on me, but with Soren it was all pain. The pleasure never came. He slowly descended the stairs with a cigarette in his hand. He made his way over to me wearing an evil grin.

"How's my little cum bucket doing today?" he asked, his voice dripping with his treacherous intentions.

"Waiting on Daddy to tell me what he wants me to do today," I said. I had been instructed to answer Soren in that manner whenever he asked me a question.

"Good, on your back, legs spread." He said coldly. I laid down on my back like he told me to and spread my legs as far as they would go. He began to roughly insert his large fingers into my vagina, which surprisingly felt good. He used his thumb to rub circles around my clit and I could feel myself begin to be aroused for the first time in a long time. He leaned down close to my face and blew a puff of smoke right into my eyes. They began to sting and burn and just before I could begin a coughing fit, Soren replaced his thumb on my clit with the tip of the lit cigarette.

The searing pain of the hot cancer stick on my most sensitive body part caused me to almost pass out from the shock. I let out a bloodcurdling scream and began to choke violently, as I had still hadn't recovered from the smoke being blown in my face. Soren began to sadistically laugh at my agony.

"You like that, don't you, you filthy bitch?" He burned the side of my face when I didn't answer him fast enough.

"AHHHH, yes!" I cried out. Of course, I didn't like it but again, it was how I was supposed to answer.

Soren spent the next half hour burning various parts of my body with the lit cigarette, concentrating on my vagina and jacking his dick off over me. When one cigarette went out he would light another one. He finished his torture session by forcing me to choke on his cock until he came all over my face and hair.

He left me in a huddled heap on the floor. The smell of my charred flesh permeated the air. I didn't know how much longer I could last like this. I never needed Q more than I needed him right now and I was praying that I got out of this situation. I made a promise to God that if he got me out of this dungeon, I was going to find my man and be the best mother and girlfriend I could be.

36

Q

I was excited because today was the day of our annual block party. It was an event that everybody around the hood loved. It gave everybody something to look forward to and be proud of in their community. I promised the block that if they held me down, everybody would eat and I was a man of my word. Kai and Sade had been huge helps in setting up the event.

Sade had definitely been a good influence on my little sister. I knew our mother could never be replaced, but you could tell that Sade brought that womanly influence that Kai had been missing all of her life, by being raised by her brother. She was even starting to dress more girly and she had cut her dreads and was rocking a curly little fro that I'm sure she was growing out to appear more feminine.

"Where do you want me to put these balloons, Q?" Kai asked as she walked past me holding a large arrangement of red balloons in the shape of a B.

"Tie them on the stop sign over there," I told her.

Just then Sade walked past me, holding her camera in one hand and bag of paper plates in the other. "Look at you being all obedient and doing what a nigga tells you to do for a change," I said as I reached out and grabbed her to bring her into my body.

"Boy bye!" she laughed. "You're paying me to be here, ain't nobody obeying you!" she exclaimed.

"*Shiiit*," I said causing her to grin again.

She had the prettiest smile. Her smooth golden brown skin was flawless, and her teeth were so white and straight. She even had a dimple in her right cheek when she smiled.

"Gimme kiss," I said as I poked my lips out at her.

"*Huuuh*...Okay." She faked like it was bothering her to kiss me, but planted her lips against mine, nonetheless.

She knew she loved kissing me, just as much as I loved kissing her.

"That's what I thought," I said as I smacked her hard on the ass as she walked away. Sade didn't have a whole lot of ass, but it was enough to grip when I was digging her out, and that was all I needed.

The party was finally under way and everybody was having an amazing time. Jayda and LaMar were over by the dominoes table tag teaming everybody. Apparently, they made a great team, so they were taking everybody's money.

It was good to see LaMar be happy. He thought I didn't know about him sweating Camari all these years, but I did. I never really had proof, but my gut was always telling me that something was going on between them. And I couldn't be too shocked, Camari was a hoe. She was just doing what hoes did best and LaMar was young like me and just caught up. It was water under the bridge now, as far as I was concerned.

I was sitting back watching all the old heads do the electric slide when I felt a hand slide across my shoulders and down my chest. Thinking it was Sade, I reached up and grabbed her small hand. I just so happened to glance to my left and saw that she was actually standing over by the face paint tent taking pictures of the kids once they were done.

"What the fuck?" I asked myself in confusion.

"Hey baby, I haven't heard from you in while. Don't you miss me?"

Mimi's annoying ass voice filled my ears and I immediately saw red. "Bitch, the fuck is you doing?" I asked as I removed her hand from around me like it was a poisonous snake.

"Why are you acting so brand new nigga?" she said, placing her hand on her hip.

I couldn't believe this bitch was really out here faking the funk like this. I hadn't talked to her ass since I pulled up on her the night of Peace's birthday party. I had even stopped storing my work at her parent's house. I knew better than to put myself in compromising positions, now that I had a girl and that's exactly what Mimi was.

I made the mistake of glancing over at Sade to see if she was looking this way. She seemed preoccupied with taking pictures, so she hadn't noticed my old smash all in my face.

"Oh, I see what it is," Mimi said, following my line of sight. "So, you get some new pussy and now it's 'fuck Mimi' all of a sudden!" She intentionally raised her voice hoping to catch Sade's attention.

As if on cue, Sade looked up from her camera and turned towards where the commotion was coming from, her and everybody else in attendance as well. "Just like you dawg ass niggas," she started to go in on me, when Sade walked up.

"Is everything okay here?" Sade asked.

"No, bitch it's not!" Mimi shouted turning her fury on Sade. "You need to back the fuck up off my man before I—"

CRACK!

While Mimi was busy flapping her gums, Sade hit her ass with a two piece so crucial, her head snapped back. "Oh shit!" I said placing my fist to my mouth in surprise. I knew my baby girl was feisty, but I had no idea she had hands like that. Before Mimi could even recover, Sade pounced on her like a lion to a gazelle on them nature shows and shit. She snatched up a fist full of her hair and began to rain blows down on her face and chest.

All the people at the party began to gather around the spectacle, involving my girl and my old fuck buddy. Not wanting to see Sade kill Mimi, I motioned for Lamar to help me pry Sade off of her.

When we finally got them separated, Mimi was hardly recognizable. She had two big bald patches in her head, and both of her eyes were already swelling shut. She just laid on the ground moaning. "You got knocked the fuck out!" I heard somebody say, mimicking Chris Tucker from the movie *Friday*. I would have laughed if I hadn't turned around and got shut down by the daggers Sade was shooting at me from her eyes.

"What did I say nigga? I said don't have me out here looking stupid!" she began shouting at me.

"On god, I ain't touched that bitch since we been together," I explained to her.

"She had no fucking problem bringing her ass out here trying to embarrass me. Bitches only go off what a nigga is giving them, so you must be doing something!" she continued her tirade.

"I put it on my son that I ain't been with that bitch in months!" I told her as I raised my hands in surrender.

"Yeah, nigga let me find out!" she yelled.

Suddenly, the sound of rubber burning could be heard from down the street. I realized that with all of the melee of the fight, no one was posted to watch the street corners for signs of danger.

Without warning, a back old school Chevy came roaring down the street with two masked figures hanging out the passenger side windows holding what looked like AK-47s. Inevitably, shots were fired in rapid succession.

TAT! TAT! TAT! TAT! TAT! TAT! TAT!

People began to run for cover screaming, and yelling. I saw women grabbing children and shield their little bodies with their own. I wasted no time throwing Sade behind me, as LaMar jumped to protect Jayda.

We both pulled our gats and began to return the assailants' fire. I took cover behind an overturned table, and LaMar threw the grill down, sending meat and hot coals flying everywhere. One even landed on the back of some lady's neck. As she clutched at the burning coal, she instinctively stood up and that proved to be a fatal mistake as she instantly took a bullet to the back of the head.

Screaming and crying could be heard from men, women and children. A few party goers had taken out their own guns and were busting right along with me and LaMar. That's just how bout it our hood was, no questions asked, just having each other's backs. It seemed like the shots rang out forever before there was finally relative silence. I looked around at all the chaos and carnage around me. There were several dead bodies strewn about the vacant lot that we held the party at. Some of those lifeless faces I knew well, some I just recognized from around the way.

I could hear my son crying from across the lot. I instantly took off running to find him, jumping over dead bodies, and bloodied people along the way. "Peace! Peace!" I shouted so he would know that daddy was coming for him. "Peace, I said as I picked up the trash can that he was hiding behind.

"DADDY!" he screamed loudly and reached his hands out for me to pick him up.

Before I could, I realized he was under a dead body. My heart jumped to my throat when I realized it was none other than my own little sister Kai. "KAI! Kai! Wake up man! Wake the fuck up!" I screamed as I began to violently shake her lifeless body. Her eyes were still open, and blood was pouring out of a large hole in her chest. She died shielding her nephew from the gunfire. She sacrificed her life so that my son could live.

An unspeakable rage began brewing in my heart. "NOOOOOOOOOOOOOOOO!" I let out a soul wrenching cry. LaMar came over to me and grabbed me by the shoulders. "You gotta pull it together, man. Sade needs you." He said with a distressed look on his face.

"What do you mean?" I asked him. I wasn't prepared for whatever his answer was gonna be. "Grab Peace, man, come over here." I took one last look at my little sister and closed her eyes, before I picked my son up and ran back over to where I had left Sade.

When we got there, Jayda was holding Sade in her arms, rocking back and forth on the ground. Sade's eyes were closed and her once white sundress had a large bright red, blood stain on her abdomen.

"Oh my god! Oh my god!" Jayda just kept saying over and over again. "SOMEBODY HELP US!" She screamed. "She's pregnant!" she cried out.

TO BE CONTINUED

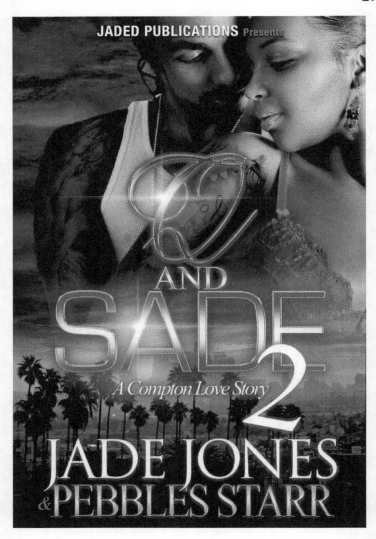

COMING SOON!!!!!

ABOUT THE AUTHOR

Jade Jones discovered her passion for creative writing in elementary school. Born in 1989, she began writing short stories and poetry as an outlet. Later on, as a teen, she led a troubled life which later resulted in her becoming a ward of the court. Jade fell in love with the art and used storytelling as a means of venting during her tumultuous times.

Aging out of the system two years later, she was thrust into the dismal world of homelessness. Desperate, and with limited income, Jade began dancing full time at the tender age of eighteen. It wasn't until Fall of 2008 when she finally caught her break after being accepted into Cleveland State University. There, Jade lived on campus and majored in Film and Television. Now, six years later, she flourishes from her childhood dream of becoming a bestselling author. Since then she has written the best-selling "Cameron" series.

Quite suitably, she uses her life's experiences to create captivating characters and story lines. Jade currently resides in Atlanta, Georgia. With no children, she spends her leisure shopping and traveling. She says that seeing new faces, meeting new people, and experiencing diverse cultures fuels her creativity. The stories are generated in her heart, the craft is practiced in her mind, and she expresses her passion through ink.

www.jadedpublications.com
https://www.facebook.com/author.jones
IG: authorjadejones
Twitter: authorjadejones
Snapchat: Jade_Jones198
Email: jade_jones89@yahoo.com